The Panther And Nine Other Amazing Short Stories

By:

W. SALVAGE

To My family…

Table of Contents:

1

The Monkey, the Shark, and the Washer-man's Donkey

Once upon a time Kee'ma, the monkey, and Pa'pa, the shark, became great friends.

The monkey lived in an immense mkooyoo tree which grew by the margin of the sea—half of its branches being over the water and half over the land.

Every morning, when the monkey was breakfasting on the kooyoo nuts, the shark would put in an appearance under

1

the tree and call out, "Throw me some food, my friend;" with which request the monkey complied most willingly.

This continued for many months, until one day Papa said, "Keema, you have done me many kindnesses: I would like you to go with me to my home, that I may repay you."

"How can I go?" said the monkey; "we land beasts can not go about in the water."

"Don't trouble yourself about that," replied the shark; "I will carry you. Not a drop of water shall get to you."

"Oh, all right, then," said Mr. Keema; "let's go."

When they had gone about half-way the shark stopped, and said: "You are my friend. I will tell you the truth."

"Why, what is there to tell?" asked the monkey, with surprise.

"Well, you see, the fact is that our sultan is very sick, and we have been told that the only medicine that will do him any good is a monkey's heart."

"Well," exclaimed Keema, "you were very foolish not to tell me that before we started!"

"How so?" asked Papa.

But the monkey was busy thinking up some means of saving himself, and made no reply.

3

"Well?" said the shark, anxiously; "why don't you speak?"

"Oh, I've nothing to say now. It's too late. But if you had told me this before we started, I might have brought my heart with me."

"What? haven't you your heart here?"

"Huh!" ejaculated Keema; "don't you know about us? When we go out we leave our hearts in the trees, and go about with only our bodies. But I see you don't believe me. You think I'm scared. Come on; let's go to your home, where you can kill me and search for my heart in vain."

The shark did believe him, though, and exclaimed, "Oh, no; let's go back and get your heart."

4

"Indeed, no," protested Keema; "let us go on to your home."

But the shark insisted that they should go back, get the heart, and start afresh.

At last, with great apparent reluctance, the monkey consented, grumbling sulkily at the unnecessary trouble he was being put to.

When they got back to the tree, he climbed up in a great hurry, calling out, "Wait there, Papa, my friend, while I get my heart, and we'll start off properly next time."

When he had got well up among the branches, he sat down and kept quite still.

After waiting what he considered a reasonable length of time, the shark called, "Come along, Keema!" But Keema just kept still and said nothing.

In a little while he called again: "Oh, Keema! let's be going."

At this the monkey poked his head out from among the upper branches and asked, in great surprise, "Going? Where?"

"To my home, of course."

"Are you mad?" queried Keema.

"Mad? Why, what do you mean?" cried Papa.

"What's the matter with you?" said the monkey. "Do you take me for a washerman's donkey?"

"What peculiarity is there about a washerman's donkey?"

"It is a creature that has neither heart nor ears."

The shark, his curiosity overcoming his haste, thereupon begged to be told the story of the washerman's donkey, which the monkey related as follows:

"A washerman owned a donkey, of which he was very fond. One day, however, it ran away, and took up its abode in the forest, where it led a lazy life, and consequently grew very fat.

"At length Soongoo'ra, the hare, by chance passed that way, and saw Poon'da, the donkey.

"Now, the hare is the most cunning of all beasts—if you look at his mouth you will see that he is always talking to himself about everything.

"So when Soongoora saw Poonda he said to himself, 'My, this donkey is fat!' Then he went and told Sim'ba, the lion.

"As Simba was just recovering from a severe illness, he was still so weak that he could not go hunting. He was consequently pretty hungry.

"Said Mr. Soongoora, 'I'll bring enough meat to-morrow for both of us to have a great feast, but you'll have to do the killing.'

"'All right, good friend,' exclaimed Simba, joyfully; 'you're very kind.'

"So the hare scampered off to the forest, found the donkey, and said to her, in his most courtly manner, 'Miss Poonda, I am sent to ask your hand in marriage.'

"'By whom?' simpered the donkey.

"'By Simba, the lion.'

"The donkey was greatly elated at this, and exclaimed: 'Let's go at once. This is a first-class offer.'

"They soon arrived at the lion's home, were cordially invited in, and sat down.

9

Soongoora gave Simba a signal with his eyebrow, to the effect that this was the promised feast, and that he would wait outside. Then he said to Poonda: 'I must leave you for a while to attend to some private business. You stay here and converse with your husband that is to be.'

"As soon as Soongoora got outside, the lion sprang at Poonda, and they had a great fight. Simba was kicked very hard, and he struck with his claws as well as his weak health would permit him. At last the donkey threw the lion down, and ran away to her home in the forest.

"Shortly after, the hare came back, and called, 'Haya! Simba! have you got it?'

"'I have not got it,' growled the lion; 'she kicked me and ran away; but I warrant

10

you I made her feel pretty sore, though I'm not strong.'

"'Oh, well,' remarked Soongoora; 'don't put yourself out of the way about it.'

"Then Soongoora waited many days, until the lion and the donkey were both well and strong, when he said: 'What do you think now, Simba? Shall I bring you your meat?'

"'Ay,' growled the lion, fiercely; 'bring it to me. I'll tear it in two pieces!'

"So the hare went off to the forest, where the donkey welcomed him and asked the news.

"'You are invited to call again and see your lover,' said Soongoora.

"'Oh, dear!' cried Poonda; 'that day you took me to him he scratched me awfully. I'm afraid to go near him now.'

"'Ah, pshaw!' said Soongoora; 'that's nothing. That's only Simba's way of caressing.'

"'Oh, well,' said the donkey, 'let's go.'

"So off they started again; but as soon as the lion caught sight of Poonda he sprang upon her and tore her in two pieces.

"When the hare came up, Simba said to him: 'Take this meat and roast it. As for myself, all I want is the heart and ears.'

"'Thanks,' said Soongoora. Then he went away and roasted the meat in a place where the lion could not see him, and he

12

took the heart and ears and hid them. Then he ate all the meat he needed, and put the rest away.

"Presently the lion came to him and said, 'Bring me the heart and ears.'

"'Where are they?' said the hare.

"'What does this mean?' growled Simba.

"'Why, didn't you know this was a washerman's donkey?'

"'Well, what's that to do with there being no heart or ears?'

"'For goodness' sake, Simba, aren't you old enough to know that if this beast had possessed a heart and ears it wouldn't have come back the second time?'

"Of course the lion had to admit that what Soongoora, the hare, said was true.

"And now," said Keema to the shark, "you want to make a washerman's donkey of me. Get out of there, and go home by yourself. You are not going to get me again, and our friendship is ended. Good-bye, Papa."

The Physician's Son and the King of the Snakes

Once there was a very learned physician, who died leaving his wife with a little baby boy, whom, when he was old enough, she named, according to his father's wish, Hassee'boo Kareem' Ed Deen'.

When the boy had been to school, and had learned to read, his mother sent him to a tailor, to learn his trade, but he could not learn it. Then he was sent to a silversmith, but he could not learn his trade either. After that he tried many trades, but could learn none of them. At last his mother said, "Well, stay at home for a while;" and that seemed to suit him.

One day he asked his mother what his father's business had been, and she told him he was a very great physician.

"Where are his books?" he asked.

"Well, it's a long time since I saw them," replied his mother, "but I think they are behind there. Look and see."

So he hunted around a little and at last found them, but they were almost ruined by insects, and he gained little from them.

At last, four of the neighbors came to his mother and said, "Let your boy go along with us and cut wood in the forest." It was their business to cut wood, load it on donkeys, and sell it in the town for making fires.

"All right," said she; "to-morrow I'll buy him a donkey, and he can start fair with you."

So the next day Hasseeboo, with his donkey, went off with those four persons, and they worked very hard and made a lot of money that day. This continued for six days, but on the seventh day it rained heavily, and they had to get under the rocks to keep dry.

Now, Hasseeboo sat in a place by himself, and, having nothing else to do, he picked up a stone and began knocking on the ground with it. To his surprise the ground gave forth a hollow sound, and he called to his companions, saying, "There seems to be a hole under here."

Upon hearing him knock again, they decided to dig and see what was the cause of the hollow sound; and they had not gone very deep before they broke into a large pit, like a well, which was filled to the top with honey.

They didn't do any firewood chopping after that, but devoted their entire attention to the collection and sale of the honey.

With a view to getting it all out as quickly as possible, they told Hasseeboo to go down into the pit and dip out the honey, while they put it in vessels and took it to town for sale. They worked for three days, making a great deal of money.

At last there was only a little honey left at the very bottom of the pit, and they told the boy to scrape that together while they went to get a rope to haul him out.

But instead of getting the rope, they decided to let him remain in the pit, and divide the money among themselves. So, when he had gathered the remainder of the honey together, and called for the rope, he received no answer; and after he had been alone in the pit for three days he became convinced that his companions had deserted him.

Then those four persons went to his mother and told her that they had become separated in the forest, that they had heard a lion roaring, and that they could find no trace of either her son or his donkey.

His mother, of course, cried very much, and the four neighbors pocketed her son's share of the money.

To return to Hasseeboo.

He passed the time walking about the pit, wondering what the end would be, eating scraps of honey, sleeping a little, and sitting down to think.

While engaged in the last occupation, on the fourth day, he saw a scorpion fall to the ground—a large one, too—and he killed it.

Then suddenly he thought to himself, "Where did that scorpion come from?

There must be a hole somewhere. I'll search, anyhow."

So he searched around until he saw light through a tiny crack; and he took his knife and scooped and scooped, until he had made a hole big enough to pass through; then he went out, and came upon a place he had never seen before.

Seeing a path, he followed it until he came to a very large house, the door of which was not fastened. So he went inside, and saw golden doors, with golden locks, and keys of pearl, and beautiful chairs inlaid with jewels and precious stones, and in a reception room he saw a couch covered with a splendid spread, upon which he lay down.

Presently he found himself being lifted off the couch and put in a chair, and heard some one saying: "Do not hurt him; wake him gently," and on opening his eyes he found himself surrounded by numbers of snakes, one of them wearing beautiful royal colors.

"Hullo!" he cried; "who are you?"

"I am Sulta'nee Waa' Neeo'ka, king of the snakes, and this is my house. Who are you?"

"I am Hasseeboo Kareem Ed Deen."

"Where do you come from?"

"I don't know where I come from, or where I'm going."

"Well, don't bother yourself just now. Let's eat; I guess you are hungry, and I know I am."

Then the king gave orders, and some of the other snakes brought the finest fruits, and they ate and drank and conversed.

When the repast was ended, the king desired to hear Hasseeboo's story; so he told him all that had happened, and then asked to hear the story of his host.

"Well," said the king of the snakes, "mine is rather a long story, but you shall hear it. A long time ago I left this place, to go and live in the mountains of Al Kaaf', for the change of air. One day I saw a stranger coming along, and I said to him, 'Where are you from?' and he said, 'I am wandering in the wilderness.' 'Whose son are you?' I asked. 'My name is Bolookee'a. My father was a sultan; and when he died I opened a small chest, inside of which I found a bag, which contained a small brass box; when I had opened this I found some writing tied up in a woolen cloth, and it was all in praise of a prophet. He was described as such a good and wonderful man, that I longed to see him; but when I made inquiries concerning him I was told he was not yet born. Then I vowed I would wander until I should see him. So I left our town, and all my property, and I am wandering, but I have not yet seen that prophet.'

"Then I said to him, 'Where do you expect to find him, if he's not yet born? Perhaps if you had some serpent's water you might keep on living until you find

24

him. But it's of no use talking about that;
the serpent's water is too far away.'

"'Well,' he said, 'good-bye. I must
wander on.' So I bade him farewell, and
he went his way.

"Now, when that man had wandered
until he reached Egypt, he met another
man, who asked him, 'Who are you?'

"'I am Bolookeea. Who are you?'

"'My name is Al Faan'. Where are you
going?'

"'I have left my home, and my property,
and I am seeking the prophet.

"'H'm!' said Al Faan; 'I can tell you of a
better occupation than looking for a man

that is not born yet. Let us go and find the king of the snakes and get him to give us a charm medicine; then we will go to King Solomon and get his rings, and we shall be able to make slaves of the genii and order them to do whatever we wish.'

"And Bolookeea said, 'I have seen the king of the snakes in the mountain of Al Kaaf.'

"'All right,' said Al Faan; 'let's go.'

"Now, Al Faan wanted the ring of Solomon that he might be a great magician and control the genii and the birds, while all Bolookeea wanted was to see the great prophet.

"As they went along, Al Faan said to Bolookeea, 'Let us make a cage and entice

26

the king of the snakes into it; then we will shut the door and carry him off.'

"'All right,' said Bolookeea.

"So they made a cage, and put therein a cup of milk and a cup of wine, and brought it to Al Kaaf; and I, like a fool, went in, drank up all the wine and became drunk. Then they fastened the door and took me away with them.

"When I came to my senses I found myself in the cage, and Bolookeea carrying me, and I said, 'The sons of Adam are no good. What do you want from me?' And they answered, 'We want some medicine to put on our feet, so that we may walk upon the water whenever it is necessary in the course of our journey.' 'Well,' said I, 'go along.'

27

"We went on until we came to a place where there were a great number and variety of trees; and when those trees saw me, they said, 'I am medicine for this;' 'I am medicine for that;' 'I am medicine for the head;' 'I am medicine for the feet;' and presently one tree said, 'If any one puts my medicine upon his feet he can walk on water.'

"When I told that to those men they said, 'That is what we want;' and they took a great deal of it.

"Then they took me back to the mountain and set me free; and we said good-bye and parted.

"When they left me, they went on their way until they reached the sea, when they put the medicine on their feet and walked

28

over. Thus they went many days, until they came near to the place of King Solomon, where they waited while Al Faan prepared his medicines.

"When they arrived at King Solomon's place, he was sleeping, and was being watched by genii, and his hand lay on his chest, with the ring on his finger.

"As Bolookeea drew near, one of the genii said to him 'Where are you going?' And he answered, 'I'm here with Al Faan; he's going to take that ring.' 'Go back,' said the genie; 'keep out of the way. That man is going to die.'

"When Al Faan had finished his preparations, he said to Bolookeea, 'Wait here for me.' Then he went forward to take the ring, when a great cry arose, and he was thrown by some unseen force a considerable distance.

"Picking himself up, and still believing in the power of his medicines, he approached the ring again, when a strong breath blew upon him and he was burnt to ashes in a moment.

"While Bolookeea was looking at all this, a voice said, 'Go your way; this wretched being is dead.' So he returned; and when he got to the sea again he put the medicine upon his feet and passed over, and continued to wander for many years.

"One morning he saw a man sitting down, and said 'Good-morning,' to which the man replied. Then Bolookeea asked him, 'Who are you?' and he answered: 'My name is Jan Shah. Who are you?' So

Bolookeea told him who he was, and asked him to tell him his history. The man, who was weeping and smiling by turns, insisted upon hearing Bolookeea's story first. After he had heard it he said:

"'Well, sit down, and I'll tell you my story from beginning to end. My name is Jan Shah, and my father is Tooeegha'mus, a great sultan. He used to go every day into the forest to shoot game; so one day I said to him, "Father, let me go with you into the forest to-day;" but he said, "Stay at home. You are better there." Then I cried bitterly, and as I was his only child, whom he loved dearly, he couldn't stand my tears, so he said: "Very well; you shall go. Don't cry."

"'Thus we went to the forest, and took many attendants with us; and when we reached the place we ate and drank, and then every one set out to hunt.

"'I and my seven slaves went on until we saw a beautiful gazelle, which we chased as far as the sea without capturing it. When the gazelle took to the water I and four of my slaves took a boat, the other three returning to my father, and we chased that gazelle until we lost sight of the shore, but we caught it and killed it. Just then a great wind began to blow, and we lost our way.

"'When the other three slaves came to my father, he asked them, "Where is your master?" and they told him about the gazelle and the boat. Then he cried, "My son is lost! My son is lost!" and returned to the town and mourned for me as one dead.

"'After a time we came to an island, where there were a great many birds. We found fruit and water, we ate and drank, and at night we climbed into a tree and slept till morning.

"'Then we rowed to a second island, and, seeing no one around, we gathered fruit, ate and drank, and climbed a tree as before. During the night we heard many savage beasts howling and roaring near us.

"'In the morning we got away as soon as possible, and came to a third island. Looking around for food, we saw a tree full of fruit like red-streaked apples; but, as we were about to pick some, we heard a voice say, "Don't touch this tree; it belongs to the king." Toward night a number of monkeys came, who seemed much pleased to see us, and they brought us all the fruit we could eat.

"'Presently I heard one of them say, "Let us make this man our sultan." Then another one said: "What's the use? They'll all run away in the morning." But a third one said, "Not if we smash their boat." Sure enough, when we started to leave in the morning, our boat was broken in pieces. So there was nothing for it but to stay there and be entertained by the monkeys, who seemed to like us very much.

"'One day, while strolling about, I came upon a great stone house, having an inscription on the door, which said, "When any man comes to this island, he will find it difficult to leave, because the monkeys desire to have a man for their king. If he looks for a way to escape, he will think there is none; but there is one outlet, which lies to the north. If you go in that direction you will come to a great plain, which is infested with lions, leopards, and snakes. You must fight all of them; and if you overcome them you can go forward. You will then come to another great plain, inhabited by ants as big as dogs; their teeth are like those of dogs, and they are very fierce. You must fight these also, and if you overcome them, the rest of the way is clear."

"'I consulted with my attendants over this information, and we came to the conclusion that, as we could only die, anyhow, we might as well risk death to gain our freedom.

"'As we all had weapons, we set forth; and when we came to the first plain we fought, and two of my slaves were killed. Then we went on to the second plain, fought again; my other two slaves were killed, and I alone escaped.

"'After that I wandered on for many days, living on whatever I could find, until at last I came to a town, where I stayed for some time, looking for employment but finding none.

"'One day a man came up to me and said, "Are you looking for work?" "I am," said I. "Come with me, then," said he; and we went to his house.

"'When we got there he produced a camel's skin, and said, "I shall put you in this skin, and a great bird will carry you to the top of yonder mountain. When he gets you there, he will tear this skin off you. You must then drive him away and push down the precious stones you will find there. When they are all down, I will get you down."

"'So he put me in the skin; the bird carried me to the top of the mountain and was about to eat me, when I jumped up, scared him away, and then pushed down many precious stones. Then I called out to the man to take me down, but he never answered me, and went away.

"'I gave myself up for a dead man, but went wandering about, until at last, after passing many days in a great forest, I came to a house, all by itself; the old man who lived in it gave me food and drink, and I was revived.

"'I remained there a long time, and that old man loved me as if I were his own son.

"'One day he went away, and giving me the keys, told me I could open the door of every room except one which he pointed out to me.

"'Of course, when he was gone, this was the first door I opened. I saw a large garden, through which a stream flowed. Just then three birds came and alighted by the side of the stream. Immediately they changed to three most beautiful women. When they had finished bathing, they put on their clothes, and, as I stood watching them, they changed into birds again and flew away.

"'I locked the door, and went away; but my appetite was gone, and I wandered about aimlessly. When the old man came back, he saw there was something wrong with me, and asked me what was the matter. Then I told him I had seen those beautiful maidens, that I loved one of them very much, and that if I could not marry her I should die.

"'The old man told me I could not possibly have my wish. He said the three lovely beings were the daughters of the sultan of the genii, and that their home was a journey of three years from where we then were.

"'I told him I couldn't help that. He must get her for my wife, or I should die. At last he said, "Well, wait till they come again, then hide yourself and steal the clothes of the one you love so dearly."

"'So I waited, and when they came again I stole the clothes of the youngest, whose name was Sayadaa'tee Shems.

"'When they came out of the water, this one could not find her clothes. Then I stepped forward and said, "I have them." "Ah," she begged, "give them to me, their owner; I want to go away." But I said to her, "I love you very much. I want to marry you." "I want to go to my father," she replied. "You cannot go," said I.

"'Then her sisters flew away, and I took her into the house, where the old man

40

married us. He told me not to give her those clothes I had taken, but to hide them; because if she ever got them she would fly away to her old home. So I dug a hole in the ground and buried them.

"'But one day, when I was away from home, she dug them up and put them on; then, saying to the slave I had given her for an attendant, "When your master returns tell him I have gone home; if he really loves me he will follow me," she flew away.

"'When I came home they told me this, and I wandered, searching for her, many years. At last I came to a town where one asked me, "Who are you?" and I answered, "I am Jan Shah." "What was your father's name?" "Taaeeghamus." "Are you the man who married our mistress?" "Who is your mistress?" "Sayadaatee Shems." "I am he!" I cried with delight.

"'They took me to their mistress, and she brought me to her father and told him I was her husband; and everybody was happy.

"'Then we thought we should like to visit our old home, and her father's genii carried us there in three days. We stayed there a year and then returned, but in a short time my wife died. Her father tried to comfort me, and wanted me to marry another of his daughters, but I refused to be comforted, and have mourned to this day. That is my story.'

"Then Bolookeea went on his way, and wandered till he died."

Next Sultaanee Waa Neeoka said to Hasseeboo, "Now, when you go home you will do me injury."

Hasseeboo was very indignant at the idea, and said, "I could not be induced to do you an injury. Pray, send me home."

"I will send you home," said the king; "but I am sure that you will come back and kill me."

"Why, I dare not be so ungrateful," exclaimed Hasseeboo. "I swear I could not hurt you."

"Well," said the king of the snakes, "bear this in mind: when you go home, do not go to bathe where there are many people."

And he said, "I will remember." So the king sent him home, and he went to his mother's house, and she was overjoyed to find that he was not dead.

Now, the sultan of the town was very sick; and it was decided that the only thing that could cure him would be to kill the king of the snakes, boil him, and give the soup to the sultan.

For a reason known only to himself, the vizir had placed men at the public baths with this instruction: "If any one who comes to bathe here has a mark on his stomach, seize him and bring him to me."

When Hasseeboo had been home three days he forgot the warning of Sultaanee Waa Neeoka, and went to bathe with the other people. All of a sudden he was seized by some soldiers, and brought before the vizir, who said, "Take us to the home of the king of the snakes."

"I don't know where it is," said Hasseeboo.

"Tie him up," commanded the vizir.

So they tied him up and beat him until his back was all raw, and being unable to stand the pain he cried, "Let up! I will show you the place."

So he led them to the house of the king of the snakes, who, when he saw him, said, "Didn't I tell you you would come back to kill me?"

"How could I help it?" cried Hasseeboo. "Look at my back!"

"Who has beaten you so dreadfully?" asked the king.

"The vizir."

"Then there's no hope for me. But you must carry me yourself."

As they went along, the king said to Hasseeboo, "When we get to your town I shall be killed and cooked. The first skimming the vizir will offer to you, but don't you drink it; put it in a bottle and keep it. The second skimming you must drink, and you will become a great physician. The third skimming is the medicine that will cure your sultan. When the vizir asks you if you drank that first skimming say, 'I did.' Then produce the bottle containing the first, and say, 'This is the second, and it is for you.' The vizir

46

will take it, and as soon as he drinks it he will die, and both of us will have our revenge."

Everything happened as the king had said. The vizir died, the sultan recovered, and Hasseeboo was loved by all as a great physician.

The Tortoise with a Pretty Daughter

There was once a king who was very powerful. He had great influence over the wild beasts and animals. Now the tortoise was looked upon as the wisest of all beasts and men. This king had a son named Ekpenyon, to whom he gave fifty young girls as wives, but the prince did not like any of them. The king was very angry at this, and made a law that if any man had a daughter who was finer than the prince's wives, and who found favour in his son's eyes, the girl herself and her father and mother should be killed.

Now about this time the tortoise and his wife had a daughter who was very beautiful. The mother thought it was not safe to keep such a fine child, as the prince might fall in love with her, so she told her husband that her daughter ought to be killed and thrown away into the bush. The tortoise, however, was unwilling, and hid her until she was three years old. One day, when both the tortoise and his wife were away on their farm, the king's son happened to be hunting near their house, and saw a bird perched on the top of the fence round the house. The bird was watching the little girl, and was so entranced with her beauty that he did not notice the prince coming. The prince shot the bird with his bow and arrow, and it dropped inside the fence, so the prince sent his servant to gather it. While the servant was looking for the bird he came across the little girl, and was so struck with her form, that he immediately returned to his master and told him what he had seen. The prince then broke down the fence and found the child, and fell in love with her at once. He stayed and talked with her for a long time, until at last she agreed to become his wife. He then went home, but concealed from his father the fact that he had fallen in love with the beautiful daughter of the tortoise.

But the next morning he sent for the treasurer, and got sixty pieces of cloth and three hundred rods, and sent them to the tortoise. Then in the early afternoon he went down to the tortoise's house, and told him that he wished to marry his daughter. The tortoise saw at once that

what he had dreaded had come to pass,
and that his life was in danger, so he told
the prince that if the king knew, he would
kill not only himself (the tortoise), but
also his wife and daughter. The prince
replied that he would be killed himself
before he allowed the tortoise and his wife
and daughter to be killed. Eventually,
after much argument, the tortoise
consented, and agreed to hand his
daughter to the prince as his wife when
she arrived at the proper age. Then the
prince went home and told his mother
what he had done. She was in great
distress at the thought that she would lose
her son, of whom she was very proud, as
she knew that when the king heard of his
son's disobedience he would kill him.
However, the queen, although she knew
how angry her husband would be, wanted

her son to marry the girl he had fallen in love with, so she went to the tortoise and gave him some money, clothes, yams, and palm-oil as further dowry on her son's behalf in order that the tortoise should not give his daughter to another man. For the next five years the prince was constantly with the tortoise's daughter, whose name was Adet, and when she was about to be put in the fatting house, the prince told his father that he was going to take Adet as his wife. On hearing this the king was very angry, and sent word all round his kingdom that all people should come on a certain day to the market-place to hear the palaver. When the appointed day arrived the market-place was quite full of people, and the stones belonging to the king and queen were placed in the middle of the market-place.

When the king and queen arrived all the people stood up and greeted them, and they then sat down on their stones. The king then told his attendants to bring the girl Adet before him. When she arrived the king was quite astonished at her beauty. He then told the people that he had sent for them to tell them that he was angry with his son for disobeying him and taking Adet as his wife without his knowledge, but that now he had seen her himself he had to acknowledge that she was very beautiful, and that his son had made a good choice. He would therefore forgive his son.

When the people saw the girl they agreed that she was very fine and quite worthy of being the prince's wife, and begged the king to cancel the law he had made altogether, and the king agreed; and as the law had been made under the "Egbo" law, he sent for eight Egbos, and told them that the order was cancelled throughout his kingdom, and that for the future no one would be killed who had a daughter more beautiful than the prince's wives, and gave the Egbos palm wine and money to remove the law, and sent them away. Then he declared that the tortoise's daughter, Adet, should marry his son, and he made them marry the same day. A great feast was then given which lasted for fifty days, and the king killed five cows and gave all the people plenty of foo-foo and palm-oil chop, and placed a large number of pots of palm wine in the streets for the people to drink as they liked. The women brought a big play to the king's compound, and there was singing and dancing kept up day and night during the whole time. The prince and his companions also played in the market square. When the feast was over the king gave half of his kingdom to the tortoise to rule over, and three hundred slaves to work on his farm. The prince also gave his father-in-law two hundred women and one hundred girls to work for him, so the tortoise became one of the richest men in the kingdom. The prince and his wife lived together for a good many years until the king died, when the prince ruled in his place. And all this shows that the tortoise is the wisest of all men and animals.

The Panther

Once upon a time there was a widow who had two daughters and a little son. And one day the mother said to her daughters: "Take good care of the house, for I am going to see grandmother, together with your little brother!" So the daughters promised her they would do so, and their mother went off. On her way a panther met her, and asked where she were going.

She said: "I am going with my child to see my mother."

"Will you not rest a bit?" asked the panther.

"No," said she, "it is already late, and it is a long road to where my mother lives."

But the panther did not cease urging her, and finally she gave in and sat down by the road side.

"I will comb your hair a bit," said the panther. And the woman allowed the panther to comb her hair. But as he passed his claws through her hair, he tore off a bit of her skin and devoured it.

"Stop!" cried the woman, "the way you comb my hair hurts!"

But the panther tore off a much larger piece of skin. Now the woman wanted to call for help, but the panther seized and devoured her. Then he turned on her little son and killed him too, put on the woman's clothes, and laid the child's bones, which he had not yet devoured, in her basket. After that he went to the woman's home, where her two daughters were, and called in at the door: "Open the door, daughters! Mother has come home!" But they looked out through a crack and said: "Our mother's eyes are not so large as yours!"

Then the panther said: "I have been to grandmother's house, and saw her hens laying eggs. That pleases me, and is the reason why my eyes have grown so large."

"Our mother had no spots in her face such as you have."

"Grandmother had no spare bed, so I had to sleep on the peas, and they pressed themselves into my face."

"Our mother's feet are not so large as yours."

"Stupid things! That comes from walking such a distance. Come, open the door quickly!"

Then the daughters said to each other: "It must be our mother," and they opened the door. But when the panther came in, they saw it was not really their mother after all.

At evening, when the daughters were already in bed, the panther was still gnawing the bones he had brought with him.

Then the daughters asked: "Mother, what are you eating?"

"I'm eating beets," was the answer.

Then the daughters said: "Oh, mother, give us some of your beets, too! We are so hungry!"

"No," was the reply, "I will not give you any. Now be quiet and go to sleep."

But the daughters kept on begging until the false mother gave them a little finger. And then they saw that it was their little brother's finger, and they said to each other: "We must make haste to escape else he will eat us as well." And with that they ran out of the door, climbed up into a tree in the yard, and called down to the false mother: "Come out! We can see our neighbor's son celebrating his wedding!" But it was the middle of the night.

Then the mother came out, and when she saw that they were sitting in the tree, she called out angrily: "Why, I'm not able to climb!"

The daughters said: "Get into a basket and throw us the rope and we will draw you up!"

The mother did as they said. But when the basket was half-way up, they began to swing it back and forth, and bump it against the tree. Then the false mother had to turn into a panther again, lest she fall down. And the panther leaped out of the basket, and ran away.

Gradually daylight came. The daughters climbed down, seated themselves on the doorstep, and cried for their mother. And a needle-vender came by and asked them why they were crying.

"A panther has devoured our mother and our brother," said the girls. "He has gone now, but he is sure to return and devour us as well."

Then the needle-vender gave them a pair of needles, and said: "Stick these needles in the cushion of the arm chair, with the points up." The girls thanked him and went on crying.

Soon a scorpion-catcher came by; and he asked them why they were crying. "A panther has devoured our mother and brother," said the girls. "He has gone now, but he is sure to return and devour us as well."

The man gave them a scorpion and said: "Put it behind the hearth in the kitchen." The girls thanked him and went on crying.

Then an egg-seller came by and asked them why they were crying. "A panther has devoured our mother and our brother," said the girls. "He has gone now, but he is sure to return and devour us as well."

So he gave them an egg and said: "Lay it beneath the ashes in the hearth." The girls thanked him and went on crying.

Then a dealer in turtles came by, and they told him their tale. He gave them a turtle and said: "Put it in the water-barrel in the yard." And then a man came by who sold wooden clubs. He asked them why they were crying. And they told him the whole story. Then he gave them two wooden clubs and said: "Hang them up over the door to the street." The girls thanked him and did as the men had told them.

In the evening the panther came home. He sat down in the armchair in the room. Then the needles in the cushion stuck into him. So he ran into the kitchen to light the fire and see what had jabbed him so; and then it was that the scorpion hooked his sting into his hand. And when at last the fire was burning, the egg burst and spurted into one of his eyes, which was blinded. So he ran out into the yard and dipped his hand into the water-barrel, in order to cool it; and then the turtle bit it off. And when in his pain he ran out through the door into the street, the wooden clubs fell on his head and that was the end of him.

The Bird with Nine Heads

Long, long ago, there once lived a king and a queen who had a daughter. One day, when the daughter went walking in the garden, a tremendous storm suddenly came up and carried her away with it. Now the storm had come from the bird with nine heads, who had robbed the princess, and brought her to his cave. The king did not know whither his daughter had disappeared, so he had proclaimed throughout the land: "Whoever brings back the princess may have her for his bride!"

Now a youth had seen the bird as he was carrying the princess to his cave. This cave, though, was in the middle of a sheer wall of rock. One could not climb up to it from below, nor could one climb down to it from above. And as the youth was walking around the rock, another youth came along and asked him what he was doing there. So the first youth told him that the bird with nine heads had carried off the king's daughter, and had brought her up to his cave. The other chap knew what he had to do. He called together his friends, and they lowered the youth to the cave in a basket. And when he went into the cave, he saw the king's daughter sitting there, and washing the wound of the bird with nine heads; for the hound of heaven had bitten off his tenth head, and his wound was still bleeding. The princess, however, motioned to the youth to hide, and he did so. When the king's daughter had washed his wound and bandaged it, the bird with nine heads felt so comfortable, that one after another, all his nine heads fell asleep. Then the youth stepped forth from his hiding-place, and cut off his nine heads with a sword. But the king's daughter said: "It would be best if you were hauled up first, and I came after."

"No," said the youth. "I will wait below here, until you are in safety." At first the king's daughter was not willing; yet at last she allowed herself to be persuaded, and climbed into the basket. But before she did so, she took a long pin from her hair, broke it into two halves and gave him one and kept the other. She also divided her silken kerchief with him, and told him to take good care of both her gifts. But when the other man had drawn up the king's daughter, he took her along with him, and left the youth in the cave, in spite of all his calling and pleading.

The youth now took a walk about the cave. There he saw a number of maidens, all of whom had been carried off by the bird with nine heads, and who had perished there of hunger. And on the wall hung a fish, nailed against it with four nails. When he touched the fish, the latter turned into a handsome youth, who thanked him for delivering him, and they agreed to regard each other as brothers. Soon the first youth grew very hungry. He stepped out in front of the cave to search for food, but only stones were lying there. Then, suddenly, he saw a great dragon, who was licking a stone. The youth imitated him, and before long his hunger had disappeared. He next asked the dragon how he could get away from the cave, and the dragon nodded his head in the direction of his tail, as much as to say he should seat himself upon it. So he climbed up, and in the twinkling of an eye he was down on the ground, and the dragon had disappeared. He then went on until he found a tortoise-shell full of beautiful pearls. But they were magic pearls, for if you flung them into the fire, the fire ceased to burn and if you flung them into the water, the water divided and you could walk through the midst of it. The youth took the pearls out of the tortoise-shell, and put them in his pocket. Not long after he reached the sea-shore. Here he flung a pearl into the sea, and at once the waters divided and he could see the sea-dragon. The sea-dragon cried: "Who is disturbing me here in my own kingdom?" The youth answered: "I found pearls in a tortoise-shell, and have flung one into the sea, and now the waters have divided for me."

"If that is the case," said the dragon, "then come into the sea with me and we will live there together." Then the youth recognized him for the same dragon whom he had seen in the cave. And with him was the youth with whom he had formed a bond of brotherhood: He was the dragon's son.

"Since you have saved my son and become his brother, I am your father," said the old dragon. And he entertained him hospitably with food and wine.

One day his friend said to him: "My father is sure to want to reward you. But accept no money, nor any jewels from him, but only the little gourd flask over yonder. With it you can conjure up whatever you wish."

And, sure enough, the old dragon asked him what he wanted by way of a reward, and the youth answered: "I want no money, nor any jewels. All I want is the little gourd flask over yonder."

At first the dragon did not wish to give it up, but at last he did let him have it, after all. And then the youth left the dragon's castle.

When he set his foot on dry land again he felt hungry. At once a table stood before him, covered with a fine and plenteous meal. He ate and drank. After he had gone on a while, he felt weary. And there stood an ass, waiting for him, on which he mounted. After he had ridden for a while, the ass's gait seemed too uneven, and along came a wagon, into which he climbed. But the wagon shook him up too, greatly, and he thought: "If I only had a litter! That would suit me better." No more had he thought so, than the litter came along, and he seated himself in it. And the bearers carried him to the city in which dwelt the king, the queen and their daughter.

When the other youth had brought back the king's daughter, it was decided to hold the wedding. But the king's daughter was not willing, and said: "He is not the right man. My deliverer will come and bring with him half of the long pin for my hair, and half my silken kerchief as a token." But when the youth did not appear for so long a time, and the other one pressed the king, the king grew impatient and said: "The wedding shall take place tomorrow!" Then the king's daughter went sadly through the streets of the city, and searched and searched in the hope of finding her deliverer. And this was on the very day that the litter arrived. The king's daughter saw the half of her silken handkerchief in the youth's hand, and filled with joy, she led him to her father. There he had to show his half of the long pin, which fitted the other exactly, and then the king was convinced that he was the right, true deliverer. The false bridegroom was now punished, the wedding celebrated, and they lived in peace and happiness till the end of their days.

The tongue-cut sparrow

Long, long ago in Japan there lived an old man and his wife. The old man was a good, kind-hearted, hard-working old fellow, but his wife was a regular crosspatch, who spoiled the happiness of her home by her scolding tongue. She was always grumbling about something from morning to night. The old man had for a long time ceased to take any notice of her crossness. He was out most of the day at work in the fields, and as he had no child, for his amusement when he came home, he kept a tame sparrow. He loved the little bird just as much as if she had been his child.

When he came back at night after his hard day's work in the open air it was his only pleasure to pet the sparrow, to talk to her and to teach her little tricks, which she learned very quickly. The old man would open her cage and let her fly about the room, and they would play together. Then when supper-time came, he always saved some tit-bits from his meal with which to feed his little bird.

Now one day the old man went out to chop wood in the forest, and the old woman stopped at home to wash clothes. The day before, she had made some starch, and now when she came to look for it, it was all gone; the bowl which she had filled full yesterday was quite empty.

While she was wondering who could have used or stolen the starch, down flew the pet sparrow, and bowing her little feathered head—a trick which she had been taught by her master—the pretty bird chirped and said:

"It is I who have taken the starch. I thought it was some food put out for me in that basin, and I ate it all. If I have made a mistake I beg you to forgive me! tweet, tweet, tweet!"

You see from this that the sparrow was a truthful bird, and the old woman ought to have been willing to forgive her at once when she asked her pardon so nicely. But not so.

The old woman had never loved the sparrow, and had often quarreled with her husband for keeping what she called a dirty bird about the house, saying that it only made extra work for her. Now she was only too delighted to have some cause of complaint against the pet. She scolded and even cursed the poor little bird for her bad behavior, and not content with using these harsh, unfeeling words, in a fit of rage she seized the sparrow—who all this time had spread out her wings and bowed her head before the old woman, to show how sorry she was—and fetched the scissors and cut off the poor little bird's tongue.

"I suppose you took my starch with that tongue! Now you may see what it is like to go without it!" And with these dreadful words she drove the bird away, not caring in the least what might happen to it and without the smallest pity for its suffering, so unkind was she!

The old woman, after she had driven the sparrow away, made some more rice-paste, grumbling all the time at the trouble, and after starching all her clothes, spread the things on boards to dry in the sun, instead of ironing them as they do in England.

In the evening the old man came home. As usual, on the way back he looked forward to the time when he should reach his gate and see his pet come flying and chirping to meet him, ruffling out her feathers to show her joy, and at last coming to rest on his shoulder. But to-night the old man was very disappointed, for not even the shadow of his dear sparrow was to be seen.

He quickened his steps, hastily drew off his straw sandals, and stepped on to the veranda. Still no sparrow was to be seen. He now felt sure that his wife, in one of her cross tempers, had shut the sparrow up in its cage. So he called her and said anxiously:

"Where is Suzume San (Miss Sparrow) today?"

The old woman pretended not to know at first, and answered:

"Your sparrow? I am sure I don't know. Now I come to think of it, I haven't seen her all the afternoon. I shouldn't wonder if the ungrateful bird had flown away and left you after all your petting!"

But at last, when the old man gave her no peace, but asked her again and again, insisting that she must know what had happened to his pet, she confessed all. She told him crossly how the sparrow had eaten the rice-paste she had specially made for starching her clothes, and how when the sparrow had confessed to what she had done, in great anger she had taken her scissors and cut out her tongue, and how finally she had driven the bird away and forbidden her to return to the house again.

Then the old woman showed her husband the sparrow's tongue, saying:

"Here is the tongue I cut off! Horrid little bird, why did it eat all my starch?"

"How could you be so cruel? Oh! how could you so cruel?" was all that the old man could answer. He was too kind-hearted to punish his be shrew of a wife, but he was terribly distressed at what had happened to his poor little sparrow.

"What a dreadful misfortune for my poor Suzume San to lose her tongue!" he said to himself. "She won't be able to chirp any more, and surely the pain of the cutting of it out in that rough way must have made her ill! Is there nothing to be done?"

The old man shed many tears after his cross wife had gone to sleep. While he wiped away the tears with the sleeve of his cotton robe, a bright thought comforted him: he would go and look for the sparrow on the morrow. Having decided this he was able to go to sleep at last.

The next morning he rose early, as soon as ever the day broke, and snatching a hasty breakfast, started out over the hills and through the woods, stopping at every clump of bamboos to cry:

"Where, oh where does my tongue-cut sparrow stay? Where, oh where, does my tongue-cut sparrow stay!"

He never stopped to rest for his noonday meal, and it was far on in the afternoon when he found himself near a large bamboo wood. Bamboo groves are the favorite haunts of sparrows, and there sure enough at the edge of the wood he saw his own dear sparrow waiting to welcome him. He could hardly believe his eyes for joy, and ran forward quickly to greet her. She bowed her little head and went through a number of the tricks her master had taught her, to show her pleasure at seeing her old friend again, and, wonderful to relate, she could talk as of old. The old man told her how sorry he was for all that had happened, and inquired after her tongue, wondering how she could speak so well without it. Then the sparrow opened her beak and showed him that a new tongue had grown in place of the old one, and begged him not to think any more about the past, for she was quite well now. Then the old man knew that his sparrow was a fairy, and no common bird. It would be difficult to exaggerate the old man's rejoicing now.

85

He forgot all his troubles, he forgot even how tired he was, for he had found his lost sparrow, and instead of being ill and without a tongue as he had feared and expected to find her, she was well and happy and with a new tongue, and without a sign of the ill-treatment she had received from his wife. And above all she was a fairy.

The sparrow asked him to follow her, and flying before him she led him to a beautiful house in the heart of the bamboo grove. The old man was utterly astonished when he entered the house to find what a beautiful place it was. It was built of the whitest wood, the soft cream-colored mats which took the place of carpets were the finest he had ever seen, and the cushions that the sparrow brought out for him to sit on were made of the finest silk and crape. Beautiful vases and lacquer boxes adorned the tokonoma[1] of every room.

[1] An alcove where precious objects are displayed.

The sparrow led the old man to the place of honor, and then, taking her place at a humble distance, she thanked him with many polite bows for all the kindness he had shown her for many long years.

Then the Lady Sparrow, as we will now call her, introduced all her family to the old man. This done, her daughters, robed in dainty crape gowns, brought in on beautiful old-fashioned trays a feast of all kinds of delicious foods, till the old man began to think he must be dreaming. In the middle of the dinner some of the sparrow's daughters performed a wonderful dance, called the "suzume-odori" or the "Sparrow's dance," to amuse the guest.

Never had the old man enjoyed himself so much. The hours flew by too quickly in this lovely spot, with all these fairy sparrows to wait upon him and to feast him and to dance before him.

But the night came on and the darkness reminded him that he had a long way to go and must think about taking his leave and return home. He thanked his kind hostess for her splendid entertainment, and begged her for his sake to forget all she had suffered at the hands of his cross old wife. He told the Lady Sparrow that it was a great comfort and happiness to him to find her in such a beautiful home and to know that she wanted for nothing. It was his anxiety to know how she fared and what had really happened to her that had led him to seek her. Now he knew that all was well he could return home with a light heart. If ever she wanted him for anything she had only to send for him and he would come at once.

The Lady Sparrow begged him to stay and rest several days and enjoy the change, but the old man said he must return to his old wife—who would probably be cross at his not coming home at the usual time—and to his work, and there-fore, much as he wished to do so, he could not accept her kind invitation. But now that he knew where the Lady

Sparrow lived he would come to see her whenever he had the time.

When the Lady Sparrow saw that she could not persuade the old man to stay longer, she gave an order to some of her servants, and they at once brought in two boxes, one large and the other small. These were placed before the old man, and the Lady Sparrow asked him to choose whichever he liked for a present, which she wished to give him.

The old man could not refuse this kind proposal, and he chose the smaller box, saying:

"I am now too old and feeble to carry the big and heavy box. As you are so kind as to say that I may take whichever I like,

I will choose the small one, which will be easier for me to carry."

Then the sparrows all helped him put it on his back and went to the gate to see him off, bidding him good-by with many bows and entreating him to come again whenever he had the time. Thus the old man and his pet sparrow separated quite happily, the sparrow showing not the least ill-will for all the unkindness she had suffered at the hands of the old wife. Indeed, she only felt sorrow for the old man who had to put up with it all his life.

When the old man reached home he found his wife even crosser than usual, for it was late on in the night and she had been waiting up for him for a long time.

"Where have you been all this time?" she asked in a big voice. "Why do you come back so late?"

The old man tried to pacify her by showing her the box of presents he had brought back with him, and then he told her of all that had happened to him, and how wonderfully he had been entertained at the sparrow's house.

"Now let us see what is in the box," said the old man, not giving her time to grumble again. "You must help me open it." And they both sat down before the box and opened it.

To their utter astonishment they found the box filled to the brim with gold and silver coins and many other precious things. The mats of their little cottage fairly glittered as they took out the things one by one and put them down and handled them over and over again. The old man was overjoyed at the sight of the riches that were now his. Beyond his brightest expectations was the sparrow's gift, which would enable him to give up work and live in ease and comfort the rest of his days.

He said: "Thanks to my good little sparrow! Thanks to my good little sparrow!" many times.

But the old woman, after the first moments of surprise and satisfaction at the sight of the gold and silver were over, could not suppress the greed of her wicked nature. She now began to reproach the old man for not having brought home the big box of presents, for in the innocence of his heart he had told her how he had refused the large box of presents which the sparrows had offered him, preferring the smaller one because it was light and easy to carry home.

"You silly old man," said she, "Why did you not bring the large box? Just think what we have lost. We might have had twice as much silver and gold as this. You are certainly an old fool!" she screamed, and then went to bed as angry as she could be.

The old man now wished that he had said nothing about the big box, but it was too late; the greedy old woman, not contented with the good luck which had so unexpectedly befallen them and which she so little deserved, made up her mind, if possible, to get more.

Early the next morning she got up and made the old man describe the way to the sparrow's house. When he saw what was in her mind he tried to keep her from going, but it was useless. She would not listen to one word he said. It is strange that the old woman did not feel ashamed of going to see the sparrow after the cruel way she had treated her in cutting off her tongue in a fit of rage. But her greed to get the big box made her forget everything else. It did not even enter her thoughts that the sparrows might be angry with her—as, indeed, they were—and might punish her for what she had done.

Ever since the Lady Sparrow had returned home in the sad plight in which they had first found her, weeping and bleeding from the mouth, her whole family and relations had done little else but speak of the cruelty of the old woman. "How could she," they asked each other, "inflict such a heavy punishment for such a trifling offense as that of eating some rice-paste by mistake?" They all loved the old man who was so kind and good and patient under all his troubles, but the old woman they hated, and they determined, if ever they had the chance, to punish her as she deserved. They had not long to wait.

After walking for some hours the old woman had at last found the bamboo grove which she had made her husband

96

carefully describe, and now she stood before it crying out:

"Where is the tongue-cut sparrow's house? Where is the tongue-cut sparrow's house?"

At last she saw the eaves of the house peeping out from amongst the bamboo foliage. She hastened to the door and knocked loudly.

When the servants told the Lady Sparrow that her old mistress was at the door asking to see her, she was somewhat surprised at the unexpected visit, after all that had taken place, and she wondered not a little at the boldness of the old woman in venturing to come to the house. The Lady Sparrow, however, was a polite bird, and so she went out to greet the old woman, remembering that she had once been her mistress.

The old woman intended, however, to waste no time in words, she went right to the point, without the least shame, and said:

"You need not trouble to entertain me as you did my old man. I have come myself to get the box which he so stupidly left behind. I shall soon take my leave if you will give me the big box—that is all I want!"

The Lady Sparrow at once consented, and told her servants to bring out the big box. The old woman eagerly seized it and hoisted it on her back, and without even stopping to thank the Lady Sparrow began to hurry homewards.

The box was so heavy that she could not walk fast, much less run, as she would have liked to do, so anxious was she to get home and see what was inside the box, but she had often to sit down and rest herself by the way.

While she was staggering along under the heavy load, her desire to open the box became too great to be resisted. She could wait no longer, for she supposed this big box to be full of gold and silver and precious jewels like the small one her husband had received.

At last this greedy and selfish old woman put down the box by the wayside and opened it carefully, expecting to gloat her eyes on a mine of wealth. What she saw, however, so terrified her that she nearly lost her senses. As soon as she lifted the lid, a number of horrible and frightful looking demons bounced out of the box and surrounded her as if they intended to kill her. Not even in nightmares had she ever seen such horrible creatures as her much-coveted box contained. A demon with one huge eye right in the middle of its forehead came and glared at her, monsters with gaping mouths looked as if they would devour her, a huge snake coiled and hissed about her, and a big frog hopped and croaked towards her.

The old woman had never been so frightened in her life, and ran from the spot as fast as her quaking legs would carry her, glad to escape alive. When she reached home she fell to the floor and told her husband with tears all that had happened to her, and how she had been nearly killed by the demons in the box.

Then she began to blame the sparrow, but the old man stopped her at once, saying:

"Don't blame the sparrow, it is your wickedness which has at last met with its reward. I only hope this may be a lesson to you in the future!"

The old woman said nothing more, and from that day she repented of her cross, unkind ways, and by degrees became a good old woman, so that her husband hardly knew her to be the same person, and they spent their last days together happily, free from want or care, spending carefully the treasure the old man had

received from his pet, the tongue-cut
sparrow.

The Strange Tale of Doctor Dog

Far up in the mountains of the Province of Hunan in the central part of China, there once lived in a small village a rich gentleman who had only one child. This girl, like the daughter of Kwan-yu in the story of the Great Bell, was the very joy of her father's life.

Now Mr. Min, for that was this gentleman's name, was famous throughout the whole district for his learning, and, as he was also the owner of much property, he spared no effort to teach Honeysuckle the wisdom of the sages, and to give her everything she craved. Of course this was enough to spoil most children, but Honeysuckle was not at all like other children. As sweet as the flower from which she took her name, she listened to her father's slightest command, and obeyed without ever waiting to be told a second time.

Her father often bought kites for her, of every kind and shape. There were fish, birds, butterflies, lizards and huge dragons, one of which had a tail more than thirty feet long. Mr. Min was very skilful in flying these kites for little Honeysuckle, and so naturally did his birds and butterflies circle round and hover about in the air that almost any little western boy would have been deceived and said, "Why, there is a real bird, and not a kite at all!" Then again, he would fasten a queer little instrument to the string, which made a kind of humming noise, as he waved his hand from side to side. "It is the wind singing, Daddy," cried Honeysuckle, clapping her hands with joy; "singing a kite-song to both of us." Sometimes, to teach his little darling a lesson if she had been the least naughty, Mr. Min would fasten queerly twisted scraps of paper, on which were written many Chinese words, to the string of her favourite kite.

"What are you doing, Daddy?" Honeysuckle would ask. "What can those queer-looking papers be?"

"On every piece is written a sin that we have done."

"What is a sin, Daddy?"

"Oh, when Honeysuckle has been naughty; that is a sin!" he answered gently. "Your old nurse is afraid to scold you, and if you are to grow up to be a good woman, Daddy must teach you what is right."

Then Mr. Min would send the kite up high—high over the house-tops, even higher than the tall Pagoda on the hillside. When all his cord was let out, he would pick up two sharp stones, and, handing them to Honeysuckle, would say, "Now, daughter, cut the string, and the wind will carry away the sins that are written down on the scraps of paper."

"But, Daddy, the kite is so pretty. Mayn't we keep our sins a little longer?" she would innocently ask.

"No, child; it is dangerous to hold on to one's sins. Virtue is the foundation of happiness," he would reply sternly, choking back his laughter at her question. "Make haste and cut the cord."

So Honeysuckle, always obedient—at least with her father—would saw the string in two between the sharp stones, and with a childish cry of despair would watch her favourite kite, blown by the wind, sail farther and farther away, until at last, straining her eyes, she could see it sink slowly to the earth in some far-distant meadow.

"Now laugh and be happy," Mr. Min would say, "for your sins are all gone. See that you don't get a new supply of them."

Honeysuckle was also fond of seeing the Punch and Judy show, for, you must know, this old-fashioned amusement for children was enjoyed by little folks in China, perhaps three thousand years before your great-grandfather was born. It is even said that the great Emperor, Mu, when he saw these little dancing images for the first time, was greatly enraged at seeing one of them making eyes at his favourite wife. He ordered the showman to be put to death, and it was with difficulty the poor fellow persuaded his Majesty that the dancing puppets were not really alive at all, but only images of cloth and clay.

No wonder then Honeysuckle liked to see Punch and Judy if the Son of Heaven himself had been deceived by their queer antics into thinking them real people of flesh and blood.

But we must hurry on with our story, or some of our readers will be asking, "But where is Dr. Dog? Are you never coming to the hero of this tale?" One day when Honeysuckle was sitting inside a shady pavilion that overlooked a tiny fish-pond, she was suddenly seized with a violent attack of colic. Frantic with pain, she told a servant to summon her father, and then without further ado, she fell over in a faint upon the ground.

When Mr. Min reached his daughter's side, she was still unconscious. After sending for the family physician to come post haste, he got his daughter to bed, but although she recovered from her fainting fit, the extreme pain continued until the poor girl was almost dead from exhaustion.

Now, when the learned doctor arrived and peered at her from under his gigantic spectacles, he could not discover the cause of her trouble. However, like some of our western medical men, he did not confess his ignorance, but proceeded to prescribe a huge dose of boiling water, to be followed a little later by a compound of pulverized deer's horn and dried toadskin.

Poor Honeysuckle lay in agony for three days, all the time growing weaker and weaker from loss of sleep. Every great doctor in the district had been summoned for consultation; two had come from Changsha, the chief city of the province, but all to no avail. It was one of those cases that seem to be beyond the power of even the most learned physicians. In the hope of receiving the great reward offered by the desperate father, these wise men searched from cover to cover in the great Chinese Cyclopedia of Medicine, trying in vain to find a method of treating the unhappy maiden. There was even thought of calling in a certain foreign physician from England, who was in a distant city, and was supposed, on account of some marvellous cures he had brought to pass, to be in direct league with the devil. However, the city magistrate would not allow Mr. Min to call in this outsider, for fear trouble might be stirred up among the people.

Mr. Min sent out a proclamation in every direction, describing his daughter's illness, and offering to bestow on her a handsome dowry and give her in marriage to whoever should be the means of bringing her back to health and happiness. He then sat at her bedside and waited, feeling that he had done all that was in his power. There were many answers to his invitation. Physicians, old and young, came from every part of the Empire to try their skill, and when they had seen poor Honeysuckle and also the huge pile of silver shoes her father offered as a wedding gift, they all fought with might and main for her life; some having been attracted by her great beauty and excellent reputation, others by the tremendous reward.

But, alas for poor Honeysuckle! Not one of all those wise men could cure her! One day, when she was feeling a slight change for the better, she called her father, and, clasping his hand with her tiny one said, "Were it not for your love I would give up this hard fight and pass over into the dark wood; or, as my old grandmother says, fly up into the Western Heavens. For your sake, because I am your only child, and especially because you have no son, I have struggled hard to live, but now I feel that the next attack of that dreadful pain will carry me away. And oh, I do not want to die!"

Here Honeysuckle wept as if her heart would break, and her old father wept too, for the more she suffered the more he loved her.

Just then her face began to turn pale. "It is coming! The pain is coming, father! Very soon I shall be no more. Good-bye, father! Good-bye; good——." Here her voice broke and a great sob almost broke her father's heart. He turned away from her bedside; he could not bear to see her suffer. He walked outside and sat down on a rustic bench; his head fell upon his bosom, and the great salt tears trickled down his long grey beard.

As Mr. Min sat thus overcome with grief, he was startled at hearing a low whine. Looking up he saw, to his astonishment, a shaggy mountain dog about the size of a Newfoundland. The huge beast looked into the old man's eyes with so intelligent and human an expression, with such a sad and wistful gaze, that the greybeard addressed him, saying, "Why have you come? To cure my daughter?"

The dog replied with three short barks, wagging his tail vigorously and turning toward the half-opened door that led into the room where the girl lay.

By this time, willing to try any chance whatever of reviving his daughter, Mr. Min bade the animal follow him into Honeysuckle's apartment. Placing his forepaws upon the side of her bed, the dog looked long and steadily at the wasted form before him and held his ear intently for a moment over the maiden's heart. Then, with a slight cough he deposited from his mouth into her outstretched hand, a tiny stone. Touching her wrist with his right paw, he motioned to her to swallow the stone.

"Yes, my dear, obey him," counselled her father, as she turned to him inquiringly, "for good Dr. Dog has been sent to your bedside by the mountain fairies, who have heard of your illness and who wish to invite you back to life again."

Without further delay the sick girl, who was by this time almost burned away by the fever, raised her hand to her lips and swallowed the tiny charm. Wonder of wonders! No sooner had it passed her lips than a miracle occurred. The red flush passed away from her face, the pulse resumed its normal beat, the pains departed from her body, and she arose from the bed well and smiling.

Flinging her arms about her father's neck, she cried out in joy, "Oh, I am well again; well and happy; thanks to the medicine of the good physician."

The noble dog barked three times, wild with delight at hearing these tearful words of gratitude, bowed low, and put his nose in Honeysuckle's outstretched hand.

Mr. Min, greatly moved by his daughter's magical recovery, turned to the strange physician, saying, "Noble Sir, were it not for the form you have taken, for some unknown reason, I would willingly give four times the sum in silver that I promised for the cure of the girl, into your possession. As it is, I suppose you have no use for silver, but remember that so long as we live, whatever we have is yours for the asking, and I beg of you to prolong your visit, to make this the home of your old age—in short, remain here for ever as my guest—nay, as a member of my family."

The dog barked thrice, as if in assent. From that day he was treated as an equal by father and daughter. The many servants were commanded to obey his slightest whim, to serve him with the most expensive food on the market, to spare no expense in making him the happiest and best-fed dog in all the world. Day after day he ran at Honeysuckle's side as she gathered flowers in her garden, lay down before her door when she was resting, guarded her Sedan chair when she was carried by servants into the city. In short, they were constant companions; a stranger would have thought they had been friends from childhood.

One day, however, just as they were returning from a journey outside her father's compound, at the very instant when Honeysuckle was alighting from her chair, without a moment's warning, the huge animal dashed past the attendants, seized his beautiful mistress in his mouth, and before anyone could stop him, bore her off to the mountains. By the time the alarm was sounded, darkness had fallen over the valley and as the night was cloudy no trace could be found of the dog and his fair burden.

Once more the frantic father left no stone unturned to save his daughter. Huge rewards were offered, bands of woodmen scoured the mountains high and low, but, alas, no sign of the girl could be found! The unfortunate father gave up the search and began to prepare himself for the grave. There was nothing now left in life that he cared for—nothing but thoughts of his departed daughter. Honeysuckle was gone for ever.

"Alas!" said he, quoting the lines of a famous poet who had fallen into despair:

"My whiting hair would make an endless rope,

Yet would not measure all my depth of woe."

Several long years passed by; years of sorrow for the ageing man, pining for his departed daughter. One beautiful October day he was sitting in the very same pavilion where he had so often sat with his darling. His head was bowed forward on his breast, his forehead was lined with grief. A rustling of leaves attracted his attention. He looked up. Standing directly in front of him was Dr. Dog, and lo, riding on his back, clinging to the animal's shaggy hair, was Honeysuckle, his long-lost daughter; while standing near by were three of the handsomest boys he had ever set eyes upon!

"Ah, my daughter! My darling daughter, where have you been all these years?" cried the delighted father, pressing the girl to his aching breast. "Have you suffered many a cruel pain since you were snatched away so suddenly? Has your life been filled with sorrow?"

"Only at the thought of your grief," she replied, tenderly, stroking his forehead with her slender fingers; "only at the thought of your suffering; only at the thought of how I should like to see you every day and tell you that my husband was kind and good to me. For you must know, dear father, this is no mere animal that stands beside you. This Dr. Dog, who cured me and claimed me as his bride because of your promise, is a great magician. He can change himself at will

122

into a thousand shapes. He chooses to come here in the form of a mountain beast so that no one may penetrate the secret of his distant palace."

"Then he is your husband?" faltered the old man, gazing at the animal with a new expression on his wrinkled face.

"Yes; my kind and noble husband, the father of my three sons, your grandchildren, whom we have brought to pay you a visit."

"And where do you live?"

"In a wonderful cave in the heart of the great mountains; a beautiful cave whose walls and floors are covered with crystals, and encrusted with sparkling gems. The chairs and tables are set with jewels; the rooms are lighted by a thousand glittering diamonds. Oh, it is lovelier than the palace of the Son of Heaven himself! We feed of the flesh of wild deer and mountain goats, and fish from the clearest mountain stream. We drink cold water out of golden goblets, without first boiling it, for it is purity itself. We breathe fragrant air that blows through forests of pine and hemlock. We live only to love each other and our children, and oh, we are so happy! And you, father, you must come back with us to the great mountains and live there with us the rest of your days, which, the gods grant, may be very many."

The old man pressed his daughter once more to his breast and fondled the children, who clambered over him rejoicing at the discovery of a grandfather they had never seen before.

From Dr. Dog and his fair Honeysuckle are sprung, it is said, the well-known race of people called the Yus, who even now inhabit the mountainous regions of the Canton and Hunan provinces. It is not for this reason, however, that we have told the story here, but because we felt sure every reader would like to learn the secret of the dog that cured a sick girl and won her for his bride.

The Talking Fish

Long, long before your great-grandfather was born there lived in the village of Everlasting Happiness two men called Li and Sing. Now, these two men were close friends, living together in the same house. Before settling down in the village of Everlasting Happiness they had ruled as high officials for more than twenty years. They had often treated the people very harshly, so that everybody, old and young, disliked and hated them. And yet, by robbing the wealthy merchants and by cheating the poor, these two evil companions had become rich, and it was in order to spend their ill-gotten gains in idle amusements that they sought out the village of Everlasting Happiness. "For here," said they, "we can surely find that joy which has been denied us in every other place. Here we shall no longer be scorned by men and reviled by women."

Consequently these two men bought for themselves the finest house in the village, furnished it in the most elegant manner, and decorated the walls with scrolls filled with wise sayings and pictures by famous artists. Outside there were lovely gardens filled with flowers and birds, and oh, ever so many trees with queer twisted branches growing in the shape of tigers and other wild animals.

Whenever they felt lonely Li and Sing invited rich people of the neighbourhood

127

to come and dine with them, and after they had eaten, sometimes they would go out upon the little lake in the centre of their estate, rowing in an awkward flat-bottomed boat that had been built by the village carpenter.

One day, on such an occasion, when the sun had been beating down fiercely upon the clean-shaven heads of all those on the little barge, for you must know this was long before the day when hats were worn—at least, in the village of Everlasting Happiness—Mr. Li was suddenly seized with a giddy feeling, which rapidly grew worse and worse until he was in a burning fever.

"Snake's blood mixed with powdered deer-horn is the thing for him," said the wise-looking doctor who was called in, peering at Li carefully through his huge glasses, "Be sure," he continued, addressing Li's personal attendant, and, at the same time, snapping his long finger-nails nervously, "be sure, above all, not to leave him alone, for he is in danger of going raving mad at any moment, and I cannot say what he may do if he is not looked after carefully. A man in his condition has no more sense than a baby."

Now, although these words of the doctor's really made Mr. Li angry, he was too ill to reply, for all this time his head had been growing hotter and hotter, until at last a feverish sleep overtook him. No sooner had he closed his eyes than his faithful servant, half-famished, rushed out of the room to join his fellows at their mid-day meal.

Li awoke with a start. He had slept only ten minutes. "Water, water," he moaned, "bathe my head with cold water. I am half dead with pain!" But there was no reply, for the attendant was dining happily with his fellows.

"Air, air," groaned Mr. Li, tugging at the collar of his silk shirt. "I'm dying for water. I'm starving for air. This blazing heat will kill me. It is hotter than the Fire god himself ever dreamed of making it. Wang, Wang!" clapping his hands feebly and calling to his servant, "air and water, air and water!"

But still no Wang.

At last, with the strength that is said to come from despair, Mr. Li arose from his couch and staggered toward the doorway. Out he went into the paved courtyard, and then, after only a moment's hesitation, made his way across it into a narrow passage that led into the lake garden.

"What do they care for a man when he is sick?" he muttered. "My good friend Sing is doubtless even now enjoying his afternoon nap, with a servant standing by to fan him, and a block of ice near his head to cool the air. What does he care if I die of a raging fever? Doubtless he expects to inherit all my money. And my servants! That rascal Wang has been with me these ten years, living on me and growing lazier every season! What does he care if I pass away? Doubtless he is certain that Sing's

131

servants will think of something for him to do, and he will have even less work than he has now. Water, water! I shall die if I don't soon find a place to soak myself!"

So saying, he arrived at the bank of a little brook that flowed in through a water gate at one side of the garden and emptied itself into the big fish-pond. Flinging himself down by a little stream Li bathed his hands and wrists in the cool water. How delightful! If only it were deep enough to cover his whole body, how gladly would he cast himself in and enjoy the bliss of its refreshing embrace!

For a long time he lay on the ground, rejoicing at his escape from the doctor's clutches. Then, as the fever began to rise

132

again, he sprang up with a determined cry, "What am I waiting for? I will do it. There's no one to prevent me, and it will do me a world of good. I will cast myself head first into the fish-pond. It is not deep enough near the shore to drown me if I should be too weak to swim, and I am sure it will restore me to strength and health."

He hastened along the little stream, almost running in his eagerness to reach the deeper water of the pond. He was like some small Tom Brown who had escaped from the watchful eye of the master and run out to play in a forbidden spot.

Hark! Was that a servant calling? Had Wang discovered the absence of his employer? Would he sound the alarm, and would the whole place soon be alive with men searching for the fever-stricken patient?

With one last sigh of satisfaction Li flung himself, clothes and all, into the quiet waters of the fish-pond. Now Li had been brought up in Fukien province on the seashore, and was a skilful swimmer. He dived and splashed to his heart's content, then floated on the surface. "It takes me back to my boyhood," he cried, "why, oh why, is it not the fashion to swim? I'd love to live in the water all the time and yet some of my countrymen are even more afraid than a cat of getting their feet wet. As for me, I'd give anything to stay here for ever."

"You would, eh?" chuckled a hoarse voice just under him, and then there was a sort of wheezing sound, followed by a loud burst of laughter. Mr. Li jumped as if an arrow had struck him, but when he noticed the fat, ugly monster below, his fear turned into anger. "Look here, what do you mean by giving a fellow such a start! Don't you know what the Classics say about such rudeness?"

The giant fish laughed all the louder. "What time do you suppose I have for Classics? You make me laugh till I cry!"

"But you must answer my question," cried Mr. Li, more and more persistently, forgetting for the moment that he was not trying some poor culprit for a petty crime.

"Why did you laugh? Speak out at once, fellow!"

"Well, since you are such a saucy piece," roared the other, "I will tell you. It was because you awkward creatures, who call yourselves men, the most highly civilized beings in the world, always [74] think you understand a thing fully when you have only just found out how to do it."

"You are talking about the island dwarfs, the Japanese," interrupted Mr. Li, "We Chinese seldom undertake to do anything new."

"Just hear the man!" chuckled the fish. "Now, fancy your wishing to stay in the water for ever! What do you know about water? Why you're not even provided with the proper equipment for swimming.

136

What would you do if you really lived here always?"

"What am I doing now?" spluttered Mr. Li, so angry that he sucked in a mouthful of water before he knew it.

"Floundering," retorted the other.

"Don't you see me swimming? Are those big eyes of yours made of glass?"

"Yes, I see you all right," guffawed the fish, "that's just it! I see you too well. Why you tumble about as awkwardly as a water buffalo wallowing in a mud puddle!"

Now, as Mr. Li had always considered himself an expert in water sports, he was, by this time, speechless with rage, and all he could do was to paddle feebly round

137

and round with strokes just strong enough to keep himself from sinking.

"Then, too," continued the fish, more and more calm as the other lost his temper, "you have a very poor arrangement for breathing. If I am not mistaken, at the bottom of this pond you would find yourself worse off than I should be at the top of a palm tree. What would you do to keep yourself from starving? Do you think it would be convenient if you had to flop yourself out on to the land every time you wanted a bite to eat? And yet, being a man, I doubt seriously if you would be content to take the proper food for fishes. You have hardly a single feature that would make you contented if you were to join an under-water school. Look at your clothes, too, water-soaked and heavy. Do you think them suitable to protect you from cold and sickness? Nature forgot to give you any scales. Now I'm going to tell you a joke, so you must be sure to laugh. Fishes are like grocery shops—always judged by their scales. As you haven't a sign of a scale, how will people judge you? See the point, eh? Nature gave you a skin, but forgot the outer covering, except, perhaps at the ends of your fingers and your toes You surely see by this time why I consider your idea ridiculous?"

Sure enough, in spite of his recent severe attack of fever, Mr. Li had really cooled completely off. He had never understood before what great disadvantages there were connected with being a man. Why not make use of this chance acquaintance, find out from him how to get rid of that miserable possession he had called his manhood, and gain the delights that only a fish can have? "Then, are you indeed contented with your lot?" he asked finally. "Are there not moments when you would prefer to be a man?"

"I, a man!" thundered the other, lashing the water with his tail. "How dare you suggest such a disgraceful change! Can it be that you do not know my rank? Why, my fellow, you behold in me a favourite nephew of the king!"

"Then, may it please your lordship," said Mr. Li, softly, "I should be exceedingly grateful if you would speak a kind word for me to your master. Do you think it possible that he could change me in some manner into a fish and accept me as a subject?"

"Of course!" replied the other, "all things are possible to the king. Know you not that my sovereign is a loyal descendant of the great water dragon, and, as such, can never die, but lives on and on and on, for ever and ever and ever, like the ruling house of Japan?"

"Oh, oh!" gasped Mr. Li, "even the Son of Heaven, our most worshipful emperor, cannot boast of such long years. Yes, I would give my fortune to be a follower of your imperial master."

"Then follow me," laughed the other, starting off at a rate that made the water hiss and boil for ten feet around him.

Mr. Li struggled vainly to keep up. If he had thought himself a good swimmer, he now saw his mistake and every bit of remaining pride was torn to tatters. "Please wait a moment," he cried out politely, "I beg of you to remember that I am only a man!"

"Pardon me," replied the other, "it was stupid of me to forget, especially as I had just been talking about it."

Soon they reached a sheltered inlet at the farther side of the pond. There Mr. Li saw a gigantic carp idly floating about in a shallow pool, and then lazily flirting his huge tail or fluttering his fins proudly from side to side. Attendant courtiers darted hither and thither, ready to do the master's slightest bidding. One of them, splendidly attired in royal scarlet, announced, with a downward flip of the head, the approach of the King's nephew who was leading Mr. Li to an audience with his Majesty.

"Whom have you here, my lad?" began the ruler, as his nephew, hesitating for words to explain his strange request, moved his fins nervously backwards and forwards. "Strange company, it seems to me, you are keeping these days."

"Only a poor man, most royal sir," replied the other, "who beseeches your Highness to grant him your gracious favour."

"When man asks favour of a fish,

'Tis hard to penetrate his wish—

143

He often seeks a lordly dish

To serve upon his table,"

repeated the king, smiling. "And yet, nephew, you think this fellow is really peaceably inclined and is not coming among us as a spy?"

Before his friend could answer, Mr. Li had cast himself upon his knees in the shallow water, before the noble carp, and bowed thrice, until his face was daubed with mud from the bottom of the pool. "Indeed, your Majesty, I am only a poor mortal who seeks your kindly grace. If you would but consent to receive me into your school of fishes. I would for ever be your ardent admirer and your lowly slave."

144

"In sooth, the fellow talks as if in earnest," remarked the king, after a moment's reflection, "and though the request is, perhaps, the strangest to which I have ever listened, I really see no reason why I should not turn a fishly ear. But, have the goodness first to cease your bowing. You are stirring up enough mud to plaster the royal palace of a shark."

Poor Li, blushing at the monarch's reproof, waited patiently for the answer to his request.

"Very well, so be it," cried the king impulsively, "your wish is granted. Sir Trout," turning to one of his courtiers, "bring hither a fish-skin of proper size for this ambitious fellow."

No sooner said than done. The fish-skin was slipped over Mr. Li's head, and his whole body was soon tucked snugly away in the scaly coat. Only his arms remained uncovered. In the twinkling of an eye Li felt sharp pains shoot through every part of his body. His arms began to shrivel up and his hands changed little by little until they made an excellent pair of fins, just as good as those of the king himself. As for his legs and feet, they suddenly began to stick together until, wriggle as he would, Li could not separate them. "Ah, ha!" thought he, "my kicking days are over, for my toes are now turned into a first-class tail."

"Not so fast," laughed the king, as Li, after thanking the royal personage profusely, started out to try his new fins;

"not so fast, my friend. Before you depart, perhaps I'd better give you a little friendly advice, else your new powers are likely to land you on the hook of some lucky fisherman, and you will find yourself served up as a prize of the pond."

"I will gladly listen to your lordly counsel, for the words of the Most High to his lowly slave are like pearls before sea slugs. However, as I was once a man myself I think I understand the simple tricks they use to catch us fish, and I am therefore in position to avoid trouble."

"Don't be so sure about it. 'A hungry carp often falls into danger,' as one of our sages so wisely remarked. There are two cautions I would impress upon you. One is, never, never, eat a dangling worm; no matter how tempting it looks there are sure to be horrible hooks inside. Secondly, always swim like lightning if you see a net, but in the opposite direction. Now, I will have you served your first meal out of the royal pantry, but after that, you must hunt for yourself, like every other self-respecting citizen of the watery world."

After Li had been fed with several slugs, followed by a juicy worm for dessert, and after again thanking the king and the king's nephew for their kindness, he started forth to test his tail and fins. It was no easy matter, at first, to move them properly. A single flirt of the tail, no more vigorous than those he had been used to giving with his legs, would send him whirling round and round in the water, for all the world like a living top; and when he wriggled his fins, ever so slightly, as he thought, he found himself sprawling on his back in a most ridiculous fashion for a dignified member of fishkind. It took several hours of constant practice to get the proper stroke, and then he found he could move about without being conscious of any effort. It was the easiest thing he had ever done in his life; and oh! the water was so cool and delightful! "Would that I might enjoy that endless life the poets write of!" he murmured blissfully.

Many hours passed by until at last Li was compelled to admit that, although he was not tired, he was certainly hungry. How to get something to eat? Oh! why had he not asked the friendly nephew a few simple questions? How easily his lordship might have told him the way to get a good breakfast! But alas! without such advice, it would be a whale's task to accomplish it. Hither and thither he swam, into the deep still water, and along the muddy shore; down, down to the pebbly bottom—always looking, looking for a tempting worm. He dived into the weeds and rushes, poked his nose among the lily pads. All for nothing! No fly or worm of any kind to gladden his eager eyes! Another hour passed slowly away, and all the time his hunger was growing greater and greater. Would the fish god, the mighty dragon, not grant him even one little morsel to satisfy his aching stomach, especially since, now that he was a fish, he had no way of tightening up his belt, as hungry soldiers do when they are on a forced march?

Just as Li was beginning to think he could not wriggle his tail an instant longer, and that soon, very soon, he would feel himself slipping, slipping, slipping down to the bottom of the pond to die—at that very moment, chancing to look up, he saw, oh joy! a delicious red worm dangling a few inches above his nose. The sight gave new strength to his weary fins and tail. Another minute, and he would have had the delicate morsel in his mouth, when alas! he chanced to recall the advice given him the day before by great King Carp. "No matter how tempting it looks, there are sure to be horrible hooks inside." For an instant Li hesitated. The worm floated a trifle nearer to his half-open mouth. How tempting! After all, what was a hook to a fish when he was dying? Why be a coward? Perhaps this worm was an exception to the rule, or perhaps, perhaps any thing—really a fish in such a plight as Mr. Li could not be expected to follow advice—even the advice of a real KING.

Pop! He had it in his mouth. Oh, soft morsel, worthy of a king's desire! Now he could laugh at words of wisdom, and eat whatever came before his eye. But ugh! What was that strange feeling that—Ouch! it was the fatal hook!

With one frantic jerk, and a hundred twists and turns, poor Li sought to pull away from the cruel barb that stuck so fast in the roof of his mouth. It was now too late to wish he had kept away from temptation. Better far to have starved at the bottom of the cool pond than to be jerked out by some miserable fisherman to the light and sunshine of the busy world. Nearer and nearer he approached the surface. The more he struggled the sharper grew the cruel barb. Then, with one final splash, he found himself dangling in mid-air, swinging helplessly at the end of a long line. With a chunk he fell into a flat-bottomed boat, directly on top of several smaller fish.

"Ah, a carp!" shouted a well-known voice gleefully; "the biggest fish I've caught these three moons. What good luck!"

It was the voice of old Chang, the fisherman, who had been supplying Mr. Li's table ever since that official's arrival in the village of Everlasting Happiness. Only a word of explanation, and he, Li, would be free once more to swim about where he willed. And then there should be no more barbs for him. An escaped fish fears the hook.

"I say, Chang," he began, gasping for breath, "really now, you must chuck me overboard at once, for, don't you see, I am Mr. Li, your old master. Come, hurry up about it. I'll excuse you this time for your mistake, for, of course, you had no way of knowing. Quick!"

But Chang, with a savage jerk, pulled the hook from Li's mouth, and looked idly towards the pile of glistening fish, gloating over his catch, and wondering how much money he could demand for it. He had heard nothing of Mr. Li's remarks, for Chang had been deaf since childhood.

"Quick, quick, I am dying for air," moaned poor Li, and then, with a groan, he remembered the fisherman's affliction.

By this time they had arrived at the shore, and Li, in company with his fellow victims, found himself suddenly thrown into a wicker basket. Oh, the horrors of that journey on land! Only a tiny bit of water remained in the closely-woven thing. It was all he could do to breathe.

Joy of joys! At the door of his own house he saw his good friend Sing just coming out. "Hey, Sing," he shouted, at the top of his voice, "help, help! This son of a turtle wants to murder me. He has me in here with these fish, and doesn't seem to know that I am Li, his master. Kindly order him to take me to the lake and throw me in, for it's cool there and I like the water life much better than that on land."

Li paused to hear Sing's reply, but there came not a single word.

"I beg your honour to have a look at my catch," said old Chang to Sing. "Here is the finest fish of the season. I have brought him here so that you and my honoured master, Mr. Li, may have a treat. Carp is his favourite delicacy."

"Very kind of you, my good Chang, I'm sure, but I fear poor Mr. Li will not eat fish for some time. He has a bad attack of fever."

"There's where you're wrong," shouted Li, from his basket, flopping about with all his might, to attract attention, "I'm

156

going to die of a chill. Can't you recognise your old friend? Help me out of this trouble and you may have all my money for your pains."

"Hey, what's that!" questioned Sing, attracted, as usual, by the word money. "Shades of Confucius! It sounds as if the carp were talking."

"What, a talking fish," laughed Chang. "Why, master, I've lived nigh on to sixty year, and such a fish has never come under my sight. There are talking birds and talking beasts for that matter; but talking fish, who ever heard of such a wonder? No, I think your ears must have deceived you, but this carp will surely cause talk when I get him into the kitchen. I'm sure the cook has never seen his like.

157

Oh, master! I hope you will be hungry when you sit down to this fish. What a pity Mr. Li couldn't help you to devour it!"

"Help to devour myself, eh?" grumbled poor Li, now almost dead for lack of water. "You must take me for a cannibal, or some other sort of savage."

Old Chang had now gone round the house to the servants' quarters, and, after calling out the cook, held up poor Li by the tail for the chef to inspect.

With a mighty jerk Li tore himself away and fell at the feet of his faithful cook. "Save me, save me!" he cried out in despair; "this miserable Chang is deaf and doesn't know that I am Mr. Li, his master. My fish voice is not strong enough for his hearing. Only take me back to the pond and set me free. You shall have a pension for life, wear good clothes and eat good food, all the rest of your days. Only hear me and obey! Listen, my dear cook, listen!"

"The thing seems to be talking," muttered the cook, "but such wonders cannot be. Only ignorant old women or foreigners would believe that a fish could talk." And seizing his former master by the tail, he swung him on to a table, picked up a knife, and began to whet it on a stone.

"Oh, oh!" screamed Li, "you will stick a knife into me! You will scrape off my beautiful shiny scales! You will whack off my lovely new fins! You will murder your old master!"

"Well, you won't talk much longer," growled the cook, "I'll show you a trick or two with the blade."

So saying, with a gigantic thrust, he plunged the knife deep into the body of the trembling victim.

With a shrill cry of horror and despair, Mr. Li awoke from the deep sleep into which he had fallen. His fever was gone, but he found himself trembling with fear at thought of the terrible death that had come to him in dreamland.

"Thanks be to Buddha, I am not a fish!" he cried out joyfully; "and now I shall be well enough to enjoy the feast to which Mr. Sing has bidden guests for to-morrow. But alas, now that I can eat the old fisherman's prize carp, it has changed back into myself.

"If only the good of our dreams came true,

I shouldn't mind dreaming the whole day through."

The Man who never Laughed

There was a man, of those possessed of houses and riches, who had wealth and servants and slaves and other possessions; and he departed from the world to receive the mercy of God (whose name be exalted!), leaving a young son. And when the son grew up, he took to eating and drinking, and the hearing of instruments of music and songs, and was liberal and gave gifts, and expended the riches that his father had left to him until all the wealth had gone. He then betook himself to the sale of the male black slaves, and the female slaves, and other possessions, and expended all that he had of his father's wealth and other things, and became so poor that he worked with the labourers. In this state he remained for a period of years. While he was sitting one day beneath a wall, waiting to see who would hire him, lo! a man of comely countenance and apparel drew near to him and saluted him. So the youth said to him, "O uncle, hast thou known me before now?" The man answered him, "I have not known thee, O my son, at all; but I see the traces of affluence upon thee, though thou art in this condition." The young man replied, "O uncle, what fate and destiny have ordained hath come to pass. But hast thou, O uncle, O comely-faced, any business in which to employ me?" The man said to him, "O my son, I desire to employ thee in an easy business." The youth asked, "And what is it, O uncle?" And the man answered him, "I have with me ten sheykhs in one abode, and we have no one to perform our wants. Thou shalt receive from us, of food and clothing, what will suffice thee, and shalt serve us, and thou shalt receive of us thy portion of benefits and money. Perhaps, also, God will restore to thee thine affluence by our means." The youth therefore replied, "I hear and obey." The sheykh then said to him, "I have a condition to impose upon thee." "And what is thy condition, O uncle?" asked the youth. He answered him, "O my son, it is that thou keep our secret with respect to the things that thou shalt see us do; and when thou seest us weep, that thou ask us not respecting the cause of our weeping." And the young man replied, "Well, O uncle."

So the sheykh said to him, "O my son, come with us, relying on the blessing of God (whose name be exalted!)." And the young man followed the sheykh until the latter conducted him to the bath; after which he sent a man, who brought him a comely garment of linen, and he clad him with it, and went with him to his abode and his associates. And when the young man entered, he found it to be a high mansion, with lofty angles, ample, with chambers facing one another, and saloons; and in each saloon was a fountain of water, and birds were warbling over it, and there were windows overlooking, on every side, a beautiful garden within the mansion. The sheykh conducted him into one of the chambers, and he found it decorated with coloured marbles, and its ceiling ornamented with blue and brilliant gold, and it was spread with carpets of silk; and he found in it ten sheykhs sitting facing one another, wearing the garments of mourning, weeping, and wailing. So the young man wondered at their case, and was about to question the sheykh who had brought him, but he remembered the condition, and therefore withheld his tongue. Then the sheykh committed to the young man a chest, containing thirty thousand pieces of gold, saying to him, "O my son, expend upon us out of this chest, and upon thyself, according to what is just, and be thou faithful, and take care of that wherewith I have intrusted thee." And the young man replied, "I hear and obey." He continued to expend upon them for a period of days and nights, after which one of them died; whereupon his companions took him, and washed him and shrouded him, and buried him in a garden behind the mansion. And death ceased not to take of them one after another, until there remained only the sheykh who had hired the young man. So he remained with the young man in that mansion, and there was not with them a third; and they remained thus for a period of years. Then the sheykh fell sick; and when the young man despaired of his life, he addressed him with courtesy, and was grieved for him, and said to him, "O uncle, I have served you, and not failed in your service one hour for a period of twelve years, but have acted faithfully to you, and served you according to my power and ability." The sheykh replied, "Yes, O my son, thou hast served us until these sheykhs have been taken unto God (to whom be ascribed might and glory!), and we must inevitably die." And the young man said, "O my master, thou art in a state of peril, and I desire of thee that thou inform me what hath been the cause of your weeping, and the continuance of your wailing and your mourning and your sorrow." He replied, "O my son, thou hast no concern with that, and require me not to do what I am unable; for I have begged God (whose name be exalted!) not to afflict any one with my affliction. Now if thou desire to be safe from that into which we have fallen, open not that door," and he pointed to it with his hand, and cautioned him against it; "and if thou desire that what hath befallen us should befall thee, open it, and thou wilt know the cause of that which thou hast beheld in our conduct; but thou wilt repent, when repentance will not avail thee." Then the

168

illness increased upon the sheykh, and he died; and the young man washed him with his own hands, and shrouded him, and buried him by his companions.

He remained in that place, possessing it and all the treasure; but notwithstanding this, he was uneasy, reflecting upon the conduct of the sheykhs. And while he was meditating one day upon the words of the sheykh, and his charge to him not to open the door, it occurred to his mind that he might look at it. So he went in that direction, and searched until he saw an elegant door, over which the spider had woven its webs, and upon it were four locks of steel. When he beheld it, he remembered how the sheykh had cautioned him, and he departed from it. His soul desired him to open the door, and he restrained it during a period of seven days; but on the eighth day his soul overcame him, and he said, "I must open that door, and see what will happen to me in consequence; for nothing will repel what God (whose name be exalted!) decreeth and predestineth, and no event will happen but by His will." Accordingly he arose and opened the door, after he had broken the locks. And when he had opened the door he saw a narrow passage, along which he walked for the space of three hours; and lo! he came forth upon the bank of a great river. At this the young man wondered. And he walked along the bank, looking to the right and left; and behold! a great eagle descended from the sky, and taking up the young man with its talons, it flew with him, between heaven and earth, until it conveyed him to an

170

island in the midst of the sea. There it threw him down, and departed from him.

So the young man was perplexed at his case, not knowing whither to go; but while he was sitting one day, lo! the sail of a vessel appeared to him upon the sea, like the star in the sky; wherefore the heart of the young man became intent upon the vessel, in the hope that his escape might be effected in it. He continued looking at it until it came near unto him; and when it arrived, he beheld a bark of ivory and ebony, the oars of which were of sandal-wood and aloes-wood, and the whole of it was encased with plates of brilliant gold. There were also in it ten damsels, virgins, like moons. When the damsels saw him, they landed to him from the bark, and kissed his hands, saying to him, "Thou art

171

the king, the bridegroom." Then there advanced to him a damsel who was like the shining sun in the clear sky, having in her hand a kerchief of silk, in which were a royal robe, and a crown of gold set with varieties of jacinths. Having advanced to him, she clad him and crowned him; after which the damsels carried him in their arms to the bark, and he found in it varieties of carpets of silk of divers colours. They then spread the sails, and proceeded over the depths of the sea.

"Now when I proceeded with them," says the young man, "I felt sure that this was a dream, and knew not whither they were going with me. And when they came in sight of the land, I beheld it filled with troops, the number of which none knew but God (whose perfection be extolled, and whose name be exalted!) clad in coats of mail. They brought forward to me five marked horses, with saddles of gold, set with varieties of pearls and precious stones; and I took a horse from among these and mounted it. The four others proceeded with me; and when I mounted, the ensigns and banners were set up over my head, the drums and the cymbals were beaten, and the troops disposed themselves in two divisions, right and left. I wavered in opinion as to whether I were asleep or awake, and ceased not to advance, not believing in the reality of my stately procession, but imagining that it was the result of confused dreams, until we came in sight of a verdant meadow, in which were palaces and gardens, and trees and rivers and flowers, and birds proclaiming the perfection of God, the

173

One, the Omnipotent. And now there came forth an army from among those palaces and gardens, like the torrent when it poureth down, until it filled the meadow. When the troops drew near to me, they hailed, and lo! a king advanced from among them, riding alone, preceded by some of his chief officers walking."

The king, on approaching the young man, alighted from his courser; and the young man, seeing him do so, alighted also; and they saluted each other with the most courteous salutation. Then they mounted their horses again, and the king said to the young man, "Accompany us; for thou art my guest." So the young man proceeded with him, and they conversed together, while the stately trains in orderly disposition went on before them to the palace of the king, where they alighted, and all of them entered, together with the king and the young man, the young man's hand being in the hand of the king, who thereupon seated him on the throne of gold and seated himself beside him. When the king removed the litham from his face, lo! this supposed king was a damsel, like the shining sun in the clear sky, a lady of beauty and loveliness, and elegance and perfection, and conceit and amorous dissimulation. The young man beheld vast affluence and great prosperity, and wondered at the beauty and loveliness of the damsel. Then the damsel said to him, "Know, O king, that I am the queen of this land, and all these troops that thou hast seen, including every one, whether of cavalry or infantry, are women. There are not among them any men. The men among us, in this land, till and sow and reap, employing themselves in the cultivation of the land, and the building and repairing of the towns, and in attending to the affairs of the people, by the pursuit of every kind of art and trade; but as to the women, they are the governors and magistrates and soldiers." And the young man wondered at this extremely. And while they were thus conversing, the vizier entered; and lo! she was a grey-haired old woman, having a numerous retinue, of venerable and dignified appearance; and the queen said to her, "Bring to us the Kádee and the witnesses." So the old woman went for that purpose. And the queen turned towards the young man, conversing with him and cheering him, and dispelling his fear by kind words; and, addressing him

176

courteously, she said to him, "Art thou content for me to be thy wife?" And thereupon he arose and kissed the ground before her; but she forbade him; and he replied, "O my mistress, I am less than the servants who serve thee." She then said to him, "Seest thou not these servants and soldiers and wealth and treasures and hoards?" He answered her, "Yes." And she said to him, "All these are at thy disposal; thou shalt make use of them, and give and bestow as seemeth fit to thee." Then she pointed to a closed door, and said to him, "All these things thou shalt dispose of; but this door thou shalt not open; for if thou open it, thou wilt repent, when repentance will not avail thee." Her words were not ended when the vizier, with the Kádee and the witnesses, entered, and all of them were

177

old women, with their hair spreading over their shoulders, and of venerable and dignified appearance. When they came before the queen, she ordered them to perform the ceremony of the marriage-contract. So they married her to the young man. And she prepared the banquets and collected the troops; and when they had eaten and drunk, the young man took her as his wife. And he resided with her seven years, passing the most delightful, comfortable, and agreeable life.

But he meditated one day upon opening the door, and said, "Were it not that there are within it great treasures, better than what I have seen, she had not prohibited me from opening it." He then arose and opened the door, and lo! within it was the bird that had carried him from the shore of the great river, and deposited him upon the island. When the bird beheld him, it said to him, "No welcome to a face that will never be happy!" So, when he saw it and heard its words, he fled from it; but it followed him and carried him off, and flew with him between heaven and earth for the space of an hour, and at length deposited him in the place from which it had carried him away; after which it disappeared. He thereupon sat in that place, and, returning to his reason, he reflected upon what he had seen of affluence and glory and honour, and the riding of the troops before him, and commanding and forbidding; and he wept and wailed. He remained upon the shore of the great river, where that bird had put him, for the space of two months, wishing that he might return to his wife; but while he was one night awake, mourning and meditating, some one spoke (and he heard his voice, but saw not his person), calling out, "How great were the delights! Far, far from thee is the return of what is passed! And how many therefore will be the sighs!" So when the young man heard it, he despaired of meeting again that queen, and of the return to him of the affluence in which he had been living. He then entered the mansion where the sheykhs had resided, and knew that they had experienced the like of that which had happened unto him, and that this was the cause of their weeping and their mourning; wherefore he excused them. Grief and anxiety came upon the young man, and he entered his chamber, and ceased not to weep and moan, relinquishing food and drink and pleasant scents and laughter, until he died; and he was buried by the side of the sheykhs.

The Fox and the Wolf

A fox and a wolf inhabited the same den, resorting thither together, and thus they remained a long time. But the wolf oppressed the fox; and it so happened that the fox counselled the wolf to assume benignity, and to abandon wickedness, saying to him, "If thou persevere in thine arrogance, probably God will give power over thee to a son of Adam; for he is possessed of stratagems, and artifice, and guile; he captureth the birds from the sky, and the fish from the sea, and cutteth the mountains and transporteth them; and all this he accomplisheth through his stratagems. Betake thyself, therefore, to the practice of equity, and relinquish evil

182

and oppression; for it will be more pleasant to thy taste." The wolf, however, received not his advice; on the contrary, he returned him a rough reply, saying to him, "Thou hast no right to speak on matters of magnitude and importance." He then gave the fox such a blow that he fell down senseless; and when he recovered, he smiled in the wolf's face, apologising for his shameful words, and recited these two verses:—

"If I have been faulty in my affection for you, and committed a deed of a shameful nature, I repent of my offence, and your clemency will extend to the evildoer who craveth forgiveness."

So the wolf accepted his apology, and ceased from ill-treating him, but said to him, "Speak not of that which concerneth thee not, lest thou hear that which will not please thee." The fox replied, "I hear and obey. I will abstain from that which pleaseth thee not; for the sage hath said, 'Offer not information on a subject respecting which thou art not questioned; and reply not to words when thou art not invited; leave what concerneth thee not, to attend to that which doth concern thee; and lavish not advice upon the evil, for they will recompense thee for it with evil.'"

When the wolf heard these words of the fox, he smiled in his face; but he meditated upon employing some artifice against him, and said, "I must strive to effect the destruction of this fox." As to the fox, however, he bore patiently the

184

injurious conduct of the wolf, saying within himself, "Verily, insolence and calumny occasion destruction, and betray one into perplexity; for it hath been said, 'He who is insolent suffereth injury, and he who is ignorant repenteth, and he who feareth is safe: moderation is one of the qualities of the noble, and good manners are the noblest gain.' It is advisable to behave with dissimulation towards this tyrant, and he will inevitably be overthrown." He then said to the wolf, "Verily the Lord pardoneth and becometh propitious unto His servant when he hath sinned; and I am a weak slave, and have committed a transgression in offering thee advice. Had I foreknown the pain that I have suffered from thy blow, I had known that the elephant could not withstand nor endure it; but I will not

185

complain of the pain of that blow, on account of the happiness that hath resulted unto me from it; for, if it had a severe effect upon me, its result was happiness; and the sage hath said, 'The beating inflicted by the preceptor is at first extremely grievous; but in the end it is sweeter than clarified honey!'" So the wolf said, "I forgive thine offence, and cancel thy fault; but beware of my power, and confess thyself my slave; for thou hast experienced my severity unto him who showeth me hostility." The fox, therefore, prostrated himself before him, saying to him, "May God prolong thy life, and mayest thou not cease to subdue him who opposeth thee!" And he continued to fear the wolf, and to dissemble towards him.

186

After this the fox went one day to a vineyard, and saw in its wall a breach; but he suspected it, saying unto himself, "There must be some cause for this breach, and it hath been said, 'Whoso seeth a hole in the ground, and doth not shun it, and be cautious of advancing to it boldly, exposeth himself to danger and destruction.' It is well known that some men make a figure of the fox in the vineyard, and even put before it grapes in plates, in order that a fox may see it, and advance to it, and fall into destruction. Verily I regard this breach as a snare; and it hath been said, 'Caution is the half of cleverness.' Caution requireth me to examine this breach, and to see if I can find there anything that may lead to perdition. Covetousness doth not induce me to throw myself into destruction." He then approached it, and, going round about examining it warily, beheld it; and lo! there was a deep pit, which the owner of the vineyard had dug to catch in it the wild beasts that despoiled the vines; and he observed over it a slight covering. So he drew back from it, and said, "Praise be to God that I regarded it with caution! I hope that my enemy, the wolf, who hath made my life miserable, may fall into it, so that I alone may enjoy absolute power over the vineyard, and live in it securely." Then, shaking his head, and uttering a loud laugh, he merrily sang these verses—

"Would that I beheld at the present moment in this well a wolf, Who hath long afflicted my heart, and made me drink bitterness perforce! Would that my life might be spared, and that the wolf

188

might meet his death! Then the vineyard would be free from his presence, and I should find in it my spoil."

Having finished his song, he hurried away until he came to the wolf, when he said to him, "Verily God hath smoothed for thee the way to the vineyard without fatigue. This hath happened through thy good fortune. Mayest thou enjoy, therefore, that to which God hath granted thee access, in smoothing thy way to that plunder and that abundant sustenance without any difficulty!" So the wolf said to the fox, "What is the proof of that which thou hast declared?" The fox answered, "I went to the vineyard, and found that its owner had died; and I entered the garden, and beheld the fruits shining upon the trees."

189

So the wolf doubted not the words of the fox, and in his eagerness he arose and went to the breach. His cupidity had deceived him with vain hopes, and the fox stopped and fell down behind him as one dead, applying this verse as a proverb suited to the case—

"Dost thou covet an interview with Leyla? It is covetousness that causeth the loss of men's heads."

When the wolf came to the breach, the fox said to him, "Enter the vineyard; for thou art spared the trouble of breaking down the wall of the garden, and it remaineth for God to complete the benefit." So the wolf walked forward, desiring to enter the vineyard, and when he came to the middle of the covering of the hole, he fell into it; whereupon the fox was violently excited by happiness and joy, his anxiety and grief ceased, and in merry tones he sang these verses—

"Fortune hath compassionated my case, and felt pity for the length of my torment, And granted me what I desired, and removed that which I dreaded. I will, therefore, forgive its offences committed in former times; Even the injustice it hath shown in the turning of my hair grey. There is no escape for the wolf from utter annihilation; And the vineyard is for me alone, and I have no stupid partner."

He then looked into the pit, and beheld the wolf weeping in his repentance and sorrow for himself, and the fox wept with him. So the wolf raised his head towards him, and said, "Is it from thy compassion for me that thou hast wept, O Abu-l-Hoseyn?" "No," answered the fox, "by him who cast thee into this pit; but I weep for the length of thy past life, and in my regret at thy not having fallen into this pit before the present day. Hadst thou fallen into it before I met with thee, I had experienced refreshment and ease. But thou hast been spared to the expiration of thy decreed term and known period." The wolf, however, said to him, "Go, O evildoer, to my mother, and acquaint her with that which hath happened to me; perhaps she will contrive some means for my deliverance." But the fox replied, "The excess of thy covetousness and eager desire has entrapped thee into destruction, since thou hast fallen into a pit from which thou wilt never be saved. Knowest thou not, O ignorant wolf, that the author of the proverb saith, 'He who thinks not of results will not be secure from perils?'" "O Abu-l-Hoseyn!" rejoined the wolf, "thou wast wont to manifest an affection for me, and to desire my friendship, and fear the greatness of my power. Be not, then, rancorous towards me for that which I have done unto thee; for he who hath one in his power, and yet forgiveth, will receive a recompense from God, and the poet hath said—

"'Sow good, even on an unworthy soil; for it will not be fruitless wherever it is sown. Verily, good, though it remained long buried, none will reap but him who sowed it.'"

"O most ignorant of the beasts of prey!" said the fox, "and most stupid of the wild beasts of the regions of the earth, hast thou forgotten thy haughtiness, and insolence, and pride, and thy disregarding the rights of companionship, and thy refusing to be advised by the saying of the poet?—

"'Tyrannise not, if thou hast the power to do so; for the tyrannical is in danger of revenge, Thine eye will sleep while the oppressed, wakeful, will call down curses on thee, and God's eye sleepeth not.'"

"O Abu-l-Hoseyn!" exclaimed the wolf, "be not angry with me for my former offences, for forgiveness is required of the generous, and kind conduct is among the

194

best means of enriching one's-self. How excellent is the saying of the poet—

"'Haste to do good when thou art able; for at every season thou hast not the power.'"

He continued to abase himself to the fox, and said to him, "Perhaps thou canst find some means of delivering me from destruction." But the fox replied, "O artful, guileful, treacherous wolf! hope not for deliverance; for this is the recompense of thy base conduct, and a just retaliation." Then, shaking his jaws with laughing, he recited these two verses—

"No longer attempt to beguile me; for thou wilt not attain thy object. What thou seekest from me is impossible. Thou hast sown, and reap, then, vexation."

195

"O gentle one among the beasts of prey!" resumed the wolf, "thou art in my estimation more faithful than to leave me in this pit." He then shed tears, and repeated this couplet—

"O thou whose favours to me have been many, and whose gifts have been more than can be numbered! No misfortune hath ever yet befallen me but I have found thee ready to aid me in it."

The fox replied, "O stupid enemy, how art thou reduced to humility, submissiveness, abjectness, and obsequiousness, after thy disdain, pride, tyranny, and haughtiness! I kept company with thee through fear of thine oppression, and flattered thee without a hope of conciliating thy kindness; but now terror hath affected thee, and punishment hath overtaken thee." And he recited these two verses—

"O thou who seekest to beguile! thou hast fallen in thy base intention. Taste, then, the pain of shameful calamity, and be with other wolves cut off."

The wolf still entreated him, saying, "O gentle one! speak not with the tongue of enmity, nor look with its eye; but fulfil the covenant of fellowship with me before the time for discovering a remedy shall have passed. Arise and procure for me a rope, and tie one end of it to a tree, and let down to me its other end, that I may lay hold of it. Perhaps I may so escape from my present predicament, and I will give thee all the treasures that I possess." The fox, however, replied, "Thou hast prolonged a conversation that will not procure thy liberation. Hope not, therefore, for thy escape through my means; but reflect upon thy former wicked conduct, and the perfidy and artifice which thou thoughtest to employ against me, and how near thou art to being stoned. Know that thy soul is about to quit the world, and to perish and depart from it: then wilt thou be reduced to destruction, and an evil abode is it to which thou goest!" "O Abu-l-Hoseyn!" rejoined the wolf, "be ready in returning to friendship, and be not so rancorous. Know that he who delivereth a soul from destruction hath saved it alive, and he who saveth a soul alive is as if he had saved the lives of all mankind. Follow not a course of evil, for the wise abhor it; and there is no evil more manifest than my being in this pit, drinking the suffocating pains of death, and looking upon destruction, when thou art able to deliver me from the misery into which I have fallen." But the fox exclaimed, "O thou barbarous, hard-hearted wretch! I compare thee, with respect to the fairness of thy professions and the baseness of thine intention, to the falcon with the partridge." "And what," asked the wolf, "is the story of the falcon and the partridge?"

The fox answered, "I entered a vineyard one day to eat of its grapes, and while I was there, I beheld a falcon pounce upon a partridge; but when he had captured him, the partridge escaped from him and entered his nest, and concealed himself in it; whereupon the falcon followed him,

199

calling out to him, 'O idiot! I saw thee in the desert hungry, and, feeling compassion for thee, I gathered for thee some grain, and took hold of thee that thou mightest eat; but thou fleddest from me, and I see no reason for thy flight unless it be to mortify. Show thyself, then, and take the grain that I have brought thee and eat it, and may it be light and wholesome to thee.' So when the partridge heard these words of the falcon, he believed him and came forth to him; and the falcon stuck his talons into him, and got possession of him. The partridge therefore said to him, 'Is this that of which thou saidst that thou hadst brought for me from the desert, and of which thou saidst to me, "Eat it, and may it be light and wholesome to thee?" Thou hast lied unto me; and may God make that which thou eatest of my flesh to be a mortal poison in thy stomach!' And when he had eaten it, his feathers fell off, and his strength failed, and he forthwith died."

The fox then continued, "Know, O wolf, that he who diggeth a pit for his brother soon falleth into it himself; and thou behavedst with perfidy to me first." "Cease," replied the wolf, "from addressing me with this discourse, and propounding fables, and mention not unto me my former base actions. It is enough for me to be in this miserable state, since I have fallen into a calamity for which the enemy would pity me, much more the true friend. Consider some stratagem by means of which I may save myself, and so assist me. If the doing this occasion thee trouble, thou knowest that the true friend endureth for his own true friend the severest labour, and will suffer destruction in obtaining his deliverance; and it hath been said, 'An affectionate friend is even better than a brother.' If thou procure means for my escape, I will collect for thee such things as shall be a store for thee against the time of want, and then I will teach thee extraordinary stratagems by which thou shalt make the plenteous vineyards accessible, and shalt strip the fruitful trees: so be happy and cheerful." But the fox said, laughing as he spoke, "How excellent is that which the learned have said of him who is excessively ignorant like thee!" "And what have the learned said?" asked the wolf. The fox answered, "The learned have observed that the rude in body and in disposition is far from intelligence, and nigh unto ignorance; for thine assertion, O perfidious idiot! that the true friend undergoeth trouble for the deliverance of his own true friend is just as thou hast said; but acquaint me, with thine ignorance and thy paucity of sense, how I should bear sincere friendship towards thee with thy treachery. Hast thou considered me a true friend unto thee when I am an enemy who rejoiceth in thy misfortune? These words are more severe than the piercing of arrows, if thou understand. And as to thy saying that thou wilt give me such things as will be a store for me against the time of want, and will teach me stratagems by which I shall obtain access to the plenteous vineyards and strip the fruitful trees—how is it, O guileful traitor! that thou knowest not a stratagem by means of which to save thyself from destruction? How far, then, art thou from profiting thyself, and how far am I from receiving thine advice? If thou know of stratagems, employ them to save thyself from this predicament from which I pray God to make thine escape far distant. See, then, O idiot! if thou know any stratagem, and save thyself by its means from slaughter, before thou lavish instruction upon another. But thou art like a man whom a disease attacked, and to whom there came a man suffering from the same disease to cure him, saying to him, 'Shall I cure thee of thy disease?' The first man, therefore, said to the other, 'Why hast thou not begun by curing thyself?' So he left him and went his way. And thou, O wolf, art in the same case. Remain, then, in thy place, and endure that which hath befallen thee."

Now when the wolf heard these words of the fox, he knew that he had no kindly feeling for him; so he wept for himself, and said, "I have been careless of myself; but if God deliver me from this affliction, I will assuredly repent of my overbearing conduct unto him that is weaker than I; and I will certainly wear wool, and ascend the mountains, commemorating the praises of God (whose name be exalted!) and fearing His punishment; and I will separate myself from all the other wild beasts, and verily I will feed the warriors in defence of the religion and the poor." Then he wept and lamented; and thereupon the heart of the fox was moved with tenderness for him. On hearing his humble expressions, and the words which indicated his repenting of arrogance and pride, he was affected with compassion for him, and, leaping with joy, placed himself at the brink of the pit, and sat upon his hind-legs and hung down his tail into the cavity. Upon this the wolf arose, and stretched forth his paw towards the fox's tail, and pulled him down to him; so the fox was with him in the pit. The wolf then said to him, "O fox of little compassion! wherefore didst thou rejoice in my misfortune? Now thou hast become my companion, and in my power. Thou hast fallen into the pit with me, and punishment hath quickly overtaken thee. The sages have said, 'If any one of you reproach his brother for deriving his nourishment from miserable means, he shall experience the same necessity,' and how excellent is the saying of the poet—

"'When fortune throweth itself heavily upon some, and encampeth by the side of others, Say to those who rejoice over us, "Awake: the rejoicers over us shall suffer as we have done."'"

"I must now," he continued, "hasten thy slaughter, before thou beholdest mine." So the fox said within himself, "I have fallen into the snare with this tyrant, and my present case requireth the employment of artifice and frauds. It hath been said that the woman maketh her ornaments for the day of festivity; and, in a proverb, 'I have not reserved thee, O my tear, but for the time of my difficulty!' and if I employ not some stratagem in the affair of this tyrannical wild beast, I perish inevitably. How good is the saying of the poet—

"'Support thyself by guile; for thou livest in an age whose sons are like the lions of the forest; And brandish around the spear of artifice, that the mill of subsistence may revolve; And pluck the fruits; or if they be beyond thy reach, then content thyself with herbage.'"

He then said to the wolf, "Hasten not to kill me, lest thou repent, O courageous wild beast, endowed with might and excessive fortitude! If thou delay, and consider what I am about to tell thee, thou wilt know the desire that I formed; and if thou hasten to kill me, there will be no profit to thee in thy doing so, but we shall die here together." So the wolf said, "O thou wily deceiver! how is it that thou hopest to effect my safety and thine own, that thou askest me to give thee a delay?

Acquaint me with the desire that thou formedst." The fox replied, "As to the desire that I formed, it was such as requireth thee to recompense me for it well, since, when I heard thy promises, and thy confession of thy past conduct, and thy regret at not having before repented and done good; and when I heard thy vows to abstain from injurious conduct to thy companions and others, and to relinquish the eating of the grapes and all other fruits, and to impose upon thyself the obligation of humility, and to clip thy claws and break thy dog-teeth, and to wear wool and offer sacrifice to God (whose name be exalted!) if He delivered thee from thy present state, I was affected with compassion for thee, though I was before longing for thy destruction. So when I heard thy profession of repentance, and what thou vowedst to do if God delivered thee, I felt constrained to save thee from thy present predicament. I therefore hung down my tail that thou mightest catch hold of it and make thine escape. But thou wouldst not relinquish thy habit of severity and violence, nor desire escape and safety for thyself by gentleness. On the contrary, thou didst pull me in such a way that I thought my soul had departed, so I became a companion with thee of the abode of destruction and death; and nothing will effect the escape of myself and thee but one plan. If thou approve of this plan that I have to propose, we shall both save ourselves; and after that, it will be incumbent on thee to fulfil that which thou hast vowed to do, and I will be thy companion." So the wolf said, "And what is thy proposal that I am to accept?" The fox answered, "That thou raise thyself upright; then I will place myself upon thy head, that I may approach the surface of the earth, and when I am upon its surface I will go forth and bring thee something of which to take hold, and after that thou wilt deliver thyself." But the wolf replied, "I put no confidence in thy words; for the sages have said, 'He who confideth when he should hate is in error'; and it hath been said, 'He who confideth in the faithless is deceived, and he who maketh trial of the trier will repent.' How excellent also is the saying of the poet—

"'Let not your opinion be otherwise than evil; for ill opinion is among the strongest of intellectual qualities. Nothing casteth a man into a place of danger like the practice of good, and a fair opinion!'

"And the saying of another—

"'Always hold an evil opinion, and so be safe. Whoso liveth vigilantly, his calamities will be few. Meet the enemy with a smiling and an open face; but raise for him an army in the heart to combat him.'

"And that of another—

"'The most bitter of thine enemies is the nearest whom thou trustest in: beware then of men, and associate with them wilily. Thy favourable opinion of fortune is a weakness: think evil of it, therefore, and regard it with apprehension!'"

"Verily," rejoined the fox, "an evil opinion is not commendable in every case; but a fair opinion is among the characteristics of excellence, and its result is escape from terrors. It is befitting, O wolf, that thou employ some stratagem for thine escape from the present predicament; and it will be better for us both to escape than to die. Relinquish, therefore, thine evil opinion and thy malevolence; for if thou think favourably of me, I shall not fail to do one of two things; either I shall bring thee something of which to lay hold, and thou wilt escape from thy present situation, or I shall act perfidiously towards thee, and save myself and leave thee; but this is a thing that cannot be, for I am not secured from meeting with some such affliction as that which thou hast met with, and that would

213

be the punishment of perfidy. It hath been said in a proverb, 'Fidelity is good, and perfidy is base.' It is fit, then, that thou trust in me, for I have not been ignorant of misfortunes. Delay not, therefore, to contrive our escape, for the affair is too strait for thee to prolong thy discourse upon it."

The wolf then said, "Verily, notwithstanding my little confidence in thy fidelity, I knew what was in thy heart, that thou desiredst my deliverance when thou wast convinced of my repentance; and I said within myself, 'If he be veracious in that which he asserteth, he hath made amends for his wickedness; and if he be false, he will be recompensed by his Lord.' So now I accept thy proposal to me, and if thou act perfidiously towards me, thy perfidy will be the means of thy destruction." Then the wolf raised himself upright in the pit, and took the fox upon his shoulders, so that his head reached the surface of the ground. The fox thereupon sprang from the wolf's shoulders, and found himself upon the face of the earth, when he fell down senseless. The wolf now said to him, "O my friend! forget not my case, nor delay my deliverance."

The fox, however, uttered a loud laugh, and replied, "O thou deceived! it was nothing but my jesting with thee and deriding thee that entrapped me into thy power; for when I heard thy profession of repentance, joy excited me, and I was moved with delight, and danced, and my tail hung down into the pit; so thou didst

215

pull me, and I fell by thee. Then God (whose name be exalted!) delivered me from thy hand. Wherefore, then, should I not aid in thy destruction when thou art of the associates of the devil? Know that I dreamt yesterday that I was dancing at thy wedding, and I related the dream to an interpreter, who said to me, 'Thou wilt fall into a frightful danger, and escape from it.' So I knew that my falling into thy power and my escape was the interpretation of my dream. Thou, too, knowest, O deceived idiot! that I am thine enemy. How, then, dost thou hope, with thy little sense and thine ignorance, that I will deliver thee, when thou hast heard what rude language I used? And how shall I endeavour to deliver thee, when the learned have said that by the death of the sinner are produced ease to mankind and

216

purgation of the earth? Did I not fear that I should suffer, by fidelity to thee, such affliction as would be greater than that which may result from perfidy, I would consider upon means for thy deliverance." So when the wolf heard the words of the fox, he bit his paw in repentance. He then spoke softly to him, but obtained nothing thereby. With a low voice he said to him, "Verily, you tribe of foxes are the sweetest of people in tongue, and the most pleasant in jesting, and this is jesting in thee; but every time is not convenient for sport and joking." "O idiot!" replied the fox, "jesting hath a limit which its employer transgresseth not. Think not that God will give thee possession of me after He hath delivered me from thy power." The wolf then said to him, "Thou art one in whom it is proper to desire my liberation, on account of the former brotherhood and friendship that subsisted between us; and if thou deliver me, I will certainly recompense thee well." But the fox replied, "The sages have said, 'Take not as thy brother the ignorant and wicked, for he will disgrace thee, and not honour thee; and take not as thy brother the liar, for if good proceed from thee he will hide it, and if evil proceed from thee he will publish it!' And the sages have said, 'For everything there is a stratagem, excepting death; and everything may be rectified excepting the corruption of the very essence; and everything may be repelled excepting destiny.' And as to the recompense which thou assertest that I deserve of thee, I compare thee, in thy recompensing, to the serpent fleeing from the Háwee, when a man saw her in a state of terror, and said to her, 'What is the matter with thee, O serpent?' She answered, 'I have fled from the Háwee, for he seeketh me; and if thou deliver me from him, and conceal me with thee, I will recompense thee well, and do thee every kindness.' So the man took her, to obtain the reward, and eager for the recompense, and put her into his pocket; and when the Háwee had passed and gone his way, and what she feared had quitted her, the man said to her, 'Where is the recompense, for I have saved thee from that which thou fearedst and didst dread?' The serpent answered him, 'Tell me in what member I shall bite thee; for thou knowest that we exceed not this recompense.' She then inflicted upon him a bite, from which he died. And thee, O idiot!" continued the fox, "I compare to that serpent with that man.

Hast thou not heard the saying of the poet?—

"'Trust not a person in whose heart thou hast made anger to dwell, nor think his anger hath ceased. Verily, the vipers, though smooth to the touch, show graceful motions, and hide mortal poison.'"

"O eloquent and comely-faced animal!" rejoined the wolf, "be not ignorant of my condition, and of the fear with which mankind regard me. Thou knowest that I assault the strong places, and strip the vines. Do, therefore, what I have commanded thee, and attend to me as the slave attendeth to his master." "O ignorant idiot! who seekest what is vain," exclaimed the fox, "verily I wonder at thy stupidity, and at the roughness of thy manner, in thine ordering me to serve thee and to stand before thee as though I were a slave. But thou shalt soon see what will befall thee, by the splitting of thy head with stones, and the breaking of thy treacherous dog-teeth."

The fox then stationed himself upon a mound overlooking the vineyard, and cried out incessantly to the people of the vineyard until they perceived him and came quickly to him. He remained steady before them until they drew near unto him, and unto the pit in which was the wolf, and then he fled. So the owners of the vineyard looked into the pit, and when they beheld the wolf in it, they instantly pelted him with heavy stones, and continued throwing stones and pieces of wood upon him, and piercing him with the points of spears, until they killed him, when they departed. Then the fox returned to the pit, and standing over the place of the wolf's slaughter, saw him dead; whereupon he shook his head in the excess of his joy, and recited these verses—

"Fate removed the wolf's soul, and it was snatched away. Far distant from happiness be his soul that hath perished. How long hast thou striven, Abos Tirhán, to destroy me! But now have burning calamities befallen thee. Thou hast fallen into a pit into which none shall descend without finding in it the blasts of death."
After this the fox remained in the vineyard alone, and in security, fearing no mischief.

The-End